BONANZA GIRL

Patricia Beatty

 Avyx

First published in 1962 by William Morrow and Company, Inc.; reissued by both Morrow Junior Hooks and Beech Tree Books in 1993 with changes that update the text for contemporary readers.

Printed in the United States of America.

Published by Avyx, Inc., 2013.

1 3 5 7 9 8 6 4 2
99 01 03 05 07 06 04 02 00

Library of Congress Cataloging-in-Publication Date

Beatty, Patricia, 1922-1991.
Bonanza girl / by Patricia Beatty.
Summary: A widow and her two children head for gold rush territory in Idaho, hoping to find jobs and a new life.
ISBN 978-1-887840-34-7
[1. Mines and mineral resources—Fiction. 2. Idaho—Fiction. 3. West (U.S>)—Fiction.] I. Title.
[PZ7.B380544Bo 1999]

For my husband and my daughter, Ann,

and

for my mother, Mrs. Walter M. Robbins

CONTENTS

CHAPTER 1

We Leave for the Wilds

It all began with a crash—the crash Mrs. Dillingworth's cup made when it fell into her saucer right there in the parlor of our Portland house.

"Katherine Scott!" cried out Mrs. Dillingworth, the black feathers on her bonnet quivering with shock. "Katherine Scott, you can't be thinking seriously of taking those poor fatherless children to Idaho Territory with you. Why, it's the wildest territory there is! All those rough people and desperate characters. Why, they say it's even worth your very life to go to Spokane Falls!"

So that's how it all started, and that's when I decided to write down my adventures.

Mama, who is a widow, is Mrs. James Scott of Portland, Oregon. As for me, I am Ann Katherine Scott, thirteen going on fourteen, and I have one brother, Jemmy, who is really James Turner Scott. He's ten, and he's really quite important in my story,

1

although sometimes I think life would be a lot easier for everybody if Jemmy would stay busy with his own affairs. That wouldn't be Jemmy, though.

Mrs. Dillingworth spoke up again, as she sat next to Mama at the tea table. "Katherine, dear," she exclaimed, "you can't really mean that you're going to the gold fields in Idaho Territory? Whatever in the world do you plan to do in those awful wilds? It's no place for a lady of quality. You stay right here in Oregon where you're safe and where you have friends to look after you. Do you have any idea what kind of living conditions you would find there? Why, you might even have to live in a tent!"

I felt like giggling, and probably would have, if I hadn't been so excited about the news that I could have burst wide open. And it was almost as much news to me as it was to Mrs. Dillingworth, for Mama had just broken it to Jemmy and me before she walked in.

"Now, Ada, it isn't as bad as all that," Mama said gently. "Hundreds and hundreds of people are going to Idaho Territory every single day. I've sold the house already; we'll be setting out next week."

It was hard to believe that we were really going to leave Portland and go up to Idaho Territory to the gold mines. I could hardly wait until Mrs. Dillingworth took her leave to find out more about it, and I thought she never would go. It seemed hours and hours that Jemmy and I waited in the kitchen, eating cookies.

Then we burst into the parlor and grabbed at Mama, drowning each other out as we talked.

"Now children," said Mama calmly, "sit down while we discuss this fully."

"But what will we do in Eagle City?" I asked, after we all sat down.

"Why I'll teach school again, of course," Mama said, with a smile at my silly question. "Miners do have children, don't they?"

"School!" exploded Jemmy.

"You thought you'd get rid of school if you went to Idaho Territory, didn't you?" I shot at Jemmy.

"Children," said Mama, "I'd better be honest with you, even if it is a hard burden to put on you." Here she paused for a moment, frowning. "Your papa, God bless him and rest him, didn't leave us much else beside this house and the furniture. There's no money coming in, but it goes out just the same. I can't find a suitable teaching position in Portland; we'd be poor if we stayed here. So I decided to try one of the territories. I heard your father say once that if you wanted to make your fortune in a hurry, go to a territory, spend a year or two working hard, and go back home wealthy."

"It sounds wonderful," I said, having sudden dreams of Italian cameo brooches, blue-velvet afternoon gowns with bustles, and even, someday soon, a Madam Duval corset of my own—things for which I had deep and secret longings.

"I'm going to go right upstairs and pack," Jemmy stated, getting to his feet.

"You'll be our manly protector out there, won't you, Jemmy?" Mama asked, with just a twitch of a smile.

I was so revolted at this idea that it was all I could do to keep from hooting, but the look on Jemmy's face was so serious that I didn't.

"In that case," he said, starting upstairs, "I guess I'll have to buy me a six shooter at Spokane Falls right off, won't I?"

The very next day some men arrived to take our furniture over to a neighbor's attic for storage. There was hardly anything left at all in our Portland house by the next evening—only the Shaker chairs, Mama's old rocker, and, of course, our beds and the kitchen things.

We began to pack. Jemmy, Mama, and I got down the four old horsehair trunks, filling them with blankets, sheets, towels, table linens, feather pillows, dishes, and everything else Mama could think of that didn't come along with a rented furnished house at the gold fields.

Then we attacked the carpetbags that were in our

attic. It happened that we had eight of them, because Papa and Mama had traveled a lot when they were first married. Mama remarked how very lucky we were to have so many, and that we would both see how wise it was to store things away. After all, you never did know when you might need something.

I took two bags, and Jemmy took two. Into mine I put all my heavier dresses, my wool and merino unmentionables, and all my jewelry—my little onyx brooch, my cameo pendant, and my three pairs of earbobs.

Mama made short work of her packing, although she did have to take four of the carpetbags. Then we both went to see how Jemmy was coming along, although if Mama had asked me I could have told her. Naturally he hadn't packed his wool underwear at all; there was nothing he hated more, so there it was on the bed just the way it came from the drawer. Both carpetbags were full of his treasures, and Mama dumped them on the bed. Out flopped his slingshot, his rock collection, roller skates, his one pair of long striped overalls, and piles of horrible dime novels.

Mama was very angry. She made him repack and put in his wool suits with the vests, his heavy brown-plaid ulster, his plainest shirtwaists, and naturally his high-top shoes, overshoes, black wool stockings, and all of his woolen underwear. Then she told him to discard his dime novels.

"I need 'em; I have to have 'em," Jemmy wailed at her.

"They're cheap, trashy things," Mama said firmly.

She finally gave in, though, but did insist that he take only five, which would leave room in the carpet-bag for more of his clothing. Finally, after a great struggle, he culled the dime-novel collection down to five, which he packed tenderly away at the bottom of the bag along with his strictly forbidden slingshot.

I didn't tell Mama about this, because I had my little secret, too. I had packed away a set of false bangs against the day when I would put my hair up and have my skirts down to my ankles in grown-up elegance.

So the time passed. We said our good-bys at school, and went downtown as guests of the Dillingworth family in their shiny black carriage the last night. Mama ate seafood, because she said she wouldn't see it for a long time, and you certainly couldn't trust fish and shellfish that far inland. Jemmy and I stuffed ice cream into us until Mama began to frown. We weren't at all sure that we'd see ice cream again, so we made up for missing it ahead of time.

We were to catch the train for Spokane Falls the very first thing in the morning, and none of us slept very well that night. Almost at the crack of dawn Mama came around telling us to get up, wash our faces and hands, brush our teeth, and get dressed in a hurry, because the hired carriage was due at any time.

My, but we were excited, not so much at the idea of a train trip, because we had been on trains before and had traveled as far as San Francisco when Papa was still alive, but because we were actually leaving.

We gobbled the breakfast that Mrs. Dillingworth sent over for us, and the moment we finished the last bite the hired rig arrived. Mama and I went inside the house for the last time to put on our traveling cloaks and bonnets, and Mama turned around looking at the hallway and parlor for a moment. For a while I thought she might even cry, but she just bit her lip and said, "Well, Ann Katherine, say farewell to the old house. We'll never see it again."

"Don't you feel bad about it, Mama," I told her. "We'll make our fortune at the mines, and you'll never even think of this old house again, when you see the fine new one we'll have pretty soon. Just wait and see."

And with that we went out the door and down the front steps for the last time, and the driver helped Mama and me into the rig.

Off we went, the horse clop-clop-clopping, to the railroad station, a place we'd been many times while we waited for Papa to come home on a train.

Mama told Jemmy and me to wait on those hard

7

old wooden railroad-station benches while she bought our tickets. It seemed to us that we sat there forever, but finally she came back with the tickets in her black beaded reticule purse and with the strangest expression on her face. She was half-amused and half-angry as she sat down beside us. "Why, that ticket agent acted as if I'd lost my mind when I requested three one-way tickets to Spokane Falls," she exclaimed. "And when I told him that I was going to Eagle City and that my two children were accompanying me, he seemed positively flabbergasted. Now isn't that the strangest thing? It almost makes me angry. It's certainly none of his business where we go."

"What did he say, Mama?" I asked.

"Why, he told me that Spokane Falls would be about as far as a nice lady like myself, with two children, should really go. He said, too, that nice ladies with children just don't travel to places like Eagle City."

When train time was called, we marched right past the bulging eyes of the ticket agent and took our places in the railroad car. "Well, we're on our way, children," Mama said. "You try to sleep as much as you can, so we won't be too tired when we come to Spokane Falls, and Jemmy, you keep away from the doors and the stove and kerosene lamps, and do obey the conductor."

While Mama gave Jemmy instructions he certainly had no intention of following, I looked around the railroad car and sighed. It was like every other car I'd ever seen. The seats were hard and uncomfortable and about as slick as an icy hill, and every time I squirmed a little I nearly fell off into the aisle. There were kerosene lanterns hanging from the roof, and there was a coal and wood stove at the opposite end of the car. I took off my bonnet and gloves, placed my traveling cloak on the back of the seat, and settled down as best I could.

The train followed the Columbia River, and we stared out the windows at its great rock cliffs and waterfalls, but once we left the banks of the river, there was almost nothing to see. We rode for miles and miles and hours and hours, and saw nothing at all but dry prairie land, spotted here and there with sagebrush and sand dunes. When we came to a dusty little place called Wallula, we all switched to the new Northern Pacific line, finished two years before. While our baggage was moved, Mama, Jemmy, and I crossed the tracks along with the other passengers to have a cup of tea at a dusty little restaurant.

After we had finished our tea we boarded the Northern Pacific car, which was little different from the other car, except that it was newer. Of course, we had a new conductor, who came around collecting tickets and speaking pleasantly to all the passengers.

He finally got around to us just as we finished eating the food we had brought with us from Portland.

"We'll pull into Spokane first thing in the morning," the conductor said, dropping the "Falls" part of the name. "You folks better get some rest, ma'am."

"Is the country like this all the way to Spokane Falls?" Mama asked, folding our napkins and getting ready to put away the food basket.

"I'm afraid it is; there ain't many folks settled around these parts yet," the conductor replied. He tipped his hat politely and moved on down the aisle.

"There now, wasn't he a nice man even if his grammar was atrocious?" asked Mama. "You do as the conductor says, Jemmy and Ann Katherine. Go to sleep. You heard what he just told me. Spokane Falls first thing in the morning! And heaven only knows what we'll find there, judging from everything people tell us about it!"

CHAPTER 2

Idaho Territory

Spokane Falls was a terrible shock.

The next morning we stepped off the train, rumpled, tired, and dirty, to look at the town that really wasn't much better than the little dusty places we'd seen along the way.

"It barely beats Wallula," Jemmy stated with disgust, staring at the rutted, muddy main street and the ugly wooden one-story houses that stretched along its length.

"It certainly isn't a bit like Portland," Mama agreed, holding her traveling cloak close around her, for the prairie wind blew cold on our faces. "But, children, do look at the hills. Spokane Falls does have some remarkable scenery, doesn't it?"

I shivered as I looked at the flattened purple buttes around Spokane prairie. Here it was April, and the hills still had great patches of snow on them.

"Well," Mama went on briskly, "we have to get

11

moving before we freeze to death here. We'll have time at this stop to get some breakfast, and then we'll all feel better. No matter what you say about Spokane, though, it is the jumping-off place for the mines, and it really is busy, isn't it?"

Mama was right. Even this early, Spokane was busy. All of the stores were open, and people streamed in and out, but we couldn't help but notice how few children and ladies there were. Everywhere we looked we saw bearded men coming out of the stores and throwing wooden crates into waiting buckboards. They all seemed to be in a hurry, for as soon as they had loaded their goods they climbed into their buckboards, snatched up their whips, and clattered off eastward out of town. I was shocked at how many of the men wore guns in leather holsters at their hips, while Jemmy's eyes positively bulged at the sight.

"Spokane Falls is really a boomer, isn't it?" he commented.

"It's one of the supply points for the gold fields," Mama replied. "That's why it's so busy this early in the day. It must be a very wealthy town—it does so much business. I've heard that it has a population of 800 already, even though it was founded not too long ago."

Just then Jemmy, who had crossed the street ahead

of us and who was already on the board sidewalk, cried out, "Mama, here's a place to eat!"

Mama smiled as Jemmy opened the door as he had been taught, and we both went in.

It wasn't like a Portland restaurant at all, of course, but it looked clean enough. A little waitress took our order for ham and eggs, flannel cakes, milk, and coffee, and after a long time returned with our food. When we had finished she brought Mama the bill.

"Two dollars!" Mama exclaimed, shocked. "Why, this is outrageous! This breakfast would have only cost about sixty cents in the best hotel in San Francisco."

"Yes, ma'am," said the waitress. "But you must be new here. Everything costs more in Spokane these days, what with the gold fields opening up and people coming in all the time."

"Well, it's still outrageous," Mama said. She paid the bill all the same, and when we got outside she stated, "Well, that settles that. We'll do our outfitting for the gold fields at Fort Sherman. I won't pay these terrible Spokane Falls prices. If they had been reasonable, we would have given them our business and had our baggage taken off here. I'm glad we learned quickly and got off as cheaply as we did."

She whisked us away across the street, and got us right onto the train again.

"Humph, two whole good dollars for breakfast!" Mama snorted, sitting up as straight as she could. "The very idea! What is the country coming to?"

It didn't take any time at all to get to Rathdrum, which was even less of a place than Spokane Falls. There our trunks and carpetbags were unloaded, for this was the end of the Northern Pacific line, where we were to board the stagecoach for Fort Sherman.

The dusty stagecoach was ready, so we waited while our luggage was strapped on the top, and then climbed aboard, settling ourselves along one side.

Two men with very fierce mustaches and quite rough clothing got on, and finally a lady climbed up, too, huffing and puffing and rather red-faced as if she had just been running. She was one of the most unusual persons I had ever seen. Certainly I hadn't seen anyone like her on the streets of Portland, and I just couldn't help but stare, although I knew how rude that was.

She was tall and broad and, as we were to find out, extremely strong. Her hair was as dark and curly as ours was light and straight, and her eyes were round and blue—a blue nearly as bright as her dress and traveling cloak, which were dazzling. But it was her red-straw bonnet that was most interesting of all. Never had I seen such a bonnet! It looked like a flower garden in bloom, with two purple doves resting right in the center of it. It was a most unusual bonnet, and I just couldn't pry my eyes away from it.

This lady sat across from Mama, holding a carpet-bag on her lap and beaming at us.

"Yah," she said, "but it is good to see anoder lady get on the coach, too."

It's very hard to spell the way she talked; I can't spell her accent at all. But we could tell right away that she was a foreigner.

"I am Helga Storkersen," she said. "And who are you, missus? Where do you come from?"

Mama was shocked at Helga Storkersen's forwardness, and I could tell that she didn't want to be engaged in conversation with her. But Mama felt called upon to say something, so she answered, "I am Mrs. James Scott, formerly of Portland."

"Are these your children?" Helga Storkersen asked. "Ain't they nice, though!"

"These are my children," Mama said stiffly.

"What are their names?"

"This is Ann Katherine and this is—"

"I'm Jemmy Scott," Jemmy piped up, and I could tell that he liked Helga Storkersen, bonnet and all.

Mama was embarrassed and gave Jemmy a reprimanding look, but that didn't faze Jemmy a bit.

"Where you folks bound for?" Helga Storkersen asked, jerking back and forth, as the stagecoach started off with a rattle and rumble and a shower of mud.

Mama gave up then. "The gold fields," she said, sounding worn out.

"Oh, the gold fields," the woman repeated after her. "You been there before, missus?"

"No."

"Well, let me tell you—you'll find it pretty rough up there. I had a feller who was in the gold fields once, and he told me all about it. You kiddies got a papa up there waitin' for you?"

"Nope," cried Jemmy. "We're going up to make our fortunes."

At this, one man put down his paper, stared at Jemmy, Mama, and me, muttered something that sounded like "Lord help us all," and then went back to his paper.

"No papa at all?" said Helga Storkersen, eyeing Mama's mourning dress. "Well then, you'll be needing a good strong hired girl. I'm on my way to Eagle City myself—thought maybe I'd work in an eating house there. I was the best and strongest hired girl in the whole Palouse country. I can lift a calf, and I'm open for hire. I work real cheap, and I like you folks. How about it, missus?"

"Thank you, but we don't need hired help," said Mama, even more shocked than before at Miss Stork-

ersen's bringing up such a topic in a public place—
and before two strangers.

"Oh, well, you will," Helga commented, sure of
herself. Sitting back, she took off her wild red bonnet
and set it lovingly on top of her carpetbag.

And that's the way the stagecoach trip went all
the way to Fort Sherman—a place which was also
known then as Coeur d'Alene City and Fort Coeur
d'Alene.

The country around Fort Sherman was certainly
different from the flat, treeless, hill-rimmed Spokane
prairie. After several hours' ride we had come into a
land that was almost mountainlike, the hills thickly
covered with evergreen forests.

We rattled into Fort Sherman in the middle of the
afternoon and wearily got off the stage, followed by
Helga Storkersen and the two gentlemen passengers.
The driver tossed off our carpetbags and the horsehair
trunks, which looked sad and somehow forlorn to me
as they sat in a row on top of the dried mud ruts of
the street.

"Oh, look!" shouted Jemmy, not at all concerned
with anything but his adventure. "Look at the lake!
It's the biggest one I ever saw!"

"That's Lake Coeur d'Alene," Mama told him.
"We have to cross that to get to the gold fields and
Eagle City."

"Mama," I wailed, "we aren't going to go up there today, are we? I'm so tired."

"So am I, Ann Katherine, I'm just as tired as you are. We're going to stay at a hotel and get a good night's sleep. Tomorrow we'll get outfitted and take the steamer up the lake," Mama said.

She stooped to pick up a carpetbag but found her way blocked by Helga Storkersen, who stood there smiling, holding six of our carpetbags, one in each hand and two under each arm.

"Whatever are you doing, Miss Storkersen?" Mama asked in alarm.

"I'm takin' us to the hotel," was the reply.

"Really, Miss Storkersen, I can't have this sort of thing going on," Mama complained in a tired voice.

"Don't worry about a thing, missus," Helga boomed, striding ahead. "You leave it to Helga. I'll get us all settled just fine. You wait here."

And that's just what we did. We stood in the street, too tired to argue with the determined Helga, who was back in a short time.

"Well, missus," she announced with pride, "I got us two nice rooms at the Hotel d'Landing. It's the only hotel in town, and it's clean, even if it ain't fancy."

"Us!" Mama inquired weakly.

"Sure, missus," said Helga. "A room for you folks and a room for me."

"Oh!" said Mama.

"Well, missus, I got to have somewheres to stay."

"Of course," said Mama.

"Then we'll have us some dinner. I guess I can eat my grub with you, 'cause I ain't working for you just yet," Helga went on.

"Miss Storkersen, you've been kindness itself," Mama protested limply, "but I don't need hired help, honestly."

"Sure you don't," was Helga's response. "You don't need one right now, but just wait until you get to Eagle. You'll be glad you got a good strong worker like Helga around. It ain't everybody who can lift a calf, you know. Now you ladies just get yourselves over to the hotel while I bring over the trunks," and with this, Helga picked up a trunk that Mama, Jemmy, and I together could barely have lifted.

We were too tired to argue. Mama and I obeyed Helga while she gave instructions to Jemmy, saying, "Now, sonny, you sit on these here trunks, and don't let no desperado walk off with one of them. If anybody tries to take anything you got here, you just holler for one of those soldier boys. That's what they're here for. This place ain't Portland, and we're sure lucky to have the U.S. Army around to pertect us."

Helga strode after us, while the crowd of soldiers that had gathered cheered her exploits. But they finally picked up the other pieces of luggage and carried them up to the hotel for us. Naturally Jemmy trotted admiringly at Helga's side. We made quite a parade. But I have never been so humiliated in my life.

Mama didn't seem much in the mood to do any talking at dinner, and I knew that she was worried. I could always tell when she was upset about something, and I was pretty sure that she was wondering how to get rid of Miss Storkersen without hurting her feelings. I wished that Mama didn't feel that way; I liked Helga and hoped she'd stay with us.

"Are you goin' to get supplies here in the morning, missus?" Helga asked.

"Why, yes," Mama replied. "Things were so expensive at Spokane Falls that I thought I'd buy them here where they'd be cheaper."

"They won't be no cheaper, missus," Helga warned, shaking her head.

"Oh, dear!" Mama said. "That is terrible!"

"Don't fret yourself, missus, I'll go with you to the store and see what we can do. I know somethin' about prices up around here."

"Well, thank you, Miss Storkersen," Mama said. I could tell that she was weakening and might even hire the incredible Helga after all.

"Are there Indians here?" Jemmy demanded, his eyes shining with eagerness.

"There are supposed to be about six tribes," Helga stated, "Kootenais, Shoshones, Coeur d'Alenes, Flatheads, Nez Perce, and Blackfeet."

"Blackfeet!" Jemmy exclaimed. "I've heard of them!"

"Matter of fact," Helga said, "you'll see some Indians tomorrow when you go to Eagle City. They still hang around the old mission at Cataldo Flats."

"Real Indians!" Jemmy whooped. "Real honest-to-goodness Indians!"

"Jemmy," Mama said, glancing around the little restaurant, noticing how other diners stared and smiled. "You are attracting all sorts of attention to us. Calm yourself at once."

I knew that the minute we got off the steamer, Jemmy would look for nothing but Indians and if he saw one, talk about nothing but Indians for days.

After dinner we went straight to bed. Our room wasn't so bad; it had a big bed for Mama and me of polished brass and a screened-off cot for Jemmy. It was clean, so we slept well, and Mama stated that as long as we were so close to a United States Army post, we were as safe as if we had been in our old beds at home in Portland. Just the same, though, we locked and bolted the door and shoved a heavy oak commode in front of it.

We knew that we were right on the edge of the wilds.

The steamer was due to leave at ten-thirty the next morning, so we got up early and had breakfast. Helga Storkersen was already at one of the tables, sipping what she said was her fifth cup of coffee. That's where I learned all about Swedes and their fondness for coffee, and I must say that I can't imagine how Helga can hold so much.

"We got to get a move on, missus," were Helga's first words. "We got to buy your supplies and get them loaded on the steamer by ten o'clock."

Mama, Jemmy, and I ate a hurried breakfast under Helga's prodding, and then Mama told Jemmy and me to go and pack our carpetbags while she and Miss Storkersen went out to buy supplies.

It didn't take ten minutes to put away the night things we had worn, so Jemmy and I had nothing to do. We pulled chairs up to the window of our room and sat there watching the street down below, where the gold seekers and the soldiers were going by. It wasn't too exciting; we got quite bored before we finally spotted Helga and Mama coming out of one of the stores across the street.

Mama looked cross as she hurried up the sidewalk to the hotel.

"Oh dear, Jemmy," I warned him, "Mama is upset about something. We'd better be careful what we say and do for a while."

It was only a few minutes before we heard Mama call to us to unlock the door and let her in, and Jemmy, for once, positively leaped to do what she asked.

She and Helga sailed into the room, and Mama collapsed into a chair, her face pink with anger.

"The very idea," she fumed. "The very idea! Fifty cents a pound for coffee, a dollar a pound for butter, and two dollars for a pair of shoes for Jemmy. It's frightful! I never heard of such a thing. The storekeepers here are criminals."

"Some of them sure are," Helga agreed, "but it costs a lot to ship food and things in here, missus."

"Not that much!" Mama snapped. "Whatever do people live on up in the gold fields—thin air?"

"No, missus. I had a feller up there, and he said he lived on sowbelly, bacon, and beans."

"That's horrible!" exclaimed Mama. "That diet could make a man very sick."

"Oh, it does, missus, as sick as a dog. They get scurvy and the rheumatiz real easy up there in the hills. Gallopin' consumption and pneumony, too."

"Oh dear," Mama said weakly. "Dear, oh dear!"

"We'll make out, missus," Helga went on staunchly. "We bought flour, beans, and bacon, and lots of sowbelly. And sonny here can catch trout, and venison don't cost much. Maybe it ain't too late to put in a vegetable garden. Before the steamer leaves, I'll go back to that store and buy some seeds. They'll probably cost their weight in gold dust, but they'll be worth it, missus."

"That ghastly, terrible food," wailed Mama. "And to think what a price I had to pay for it! Then the storekeeper told me that these things would cost even more in Eagle City and that it would pay me to stock up here in Fort Sherman!"

"He was right," Helga stated. "After you leave the steamer, you got to pay a penny a pound a mile to have stuff lugged to Eagle City by mule team. That's what the man told me. That's why it costs more to get outfitted up there in the gold fields."

"It's more than I can bear," Mama wailed once more.

"Well, it could be worse, missus. They used to use dog teams to drag freight in over the trails to Eagle, and *that* cost five cents a pound a mile. Mules is cheaper."

Mama just put her hands on her forehead and shivered, saying, "Don't tell me any more, Miss Storkersen. I still have to pay the hotel bill here."

"Well," Helga said, trying to soothe Mama's flustered feelings, "it's just as I always say. Whenever things I run into look bad, I tell myself, 'Helga, things could be worse.' That always makes me feel better. It sure does."

CHAPTER 3

Timothy Clover

We took the paddle-wheel steamer, and finally landed at Cataldo Flats, a place on the Coeur d'Alene River just a few miles from the north end of the lake, and went ashore with all of what Mama called our "impedimenta," meaning our supplies and our luggage.

There we saw an abandoned mission built by the Jesuit priests well over thirty years ago, and Jemmy saw his very first Indian.

Mama, Helga, and I thought the mission was inspiring, particularly when one of our fellow passengers told us that it had been built under conditions of terrible hardship with no real carpenter's tools and with no skilled help. There it stood—a large building made entirely of wood, and, we were astonished to learn, held together entirely by pegs, for the mission fathers had had no nails to work with.

I doubt if Jemmy even saw the mission; he was too busy staring at the Indians, who were camped around Cataldo Flats. Jemmy was lost in wonder. He gaped at the Indians, and the Indians gazed back at him. I had to admit that they didn't impress me much. They certainly weren't dressed to fit the pictures we had seen. They did wear some buckskin clothing, to be sure, but I think that I saw far more calico than buckskin. There wasn't even a feather in the lot, although some of the calico-garbed women did wear beaded moccasins instead of shoes, and all of the men had long braids under their high-crowned black hats. It didn't matter to Jemmy, though; these were Indians.

Mama shook him to keep him from staring, while Helga led the way over to the waiting mule teams and riding horses.

There were several trains of mules there, waiting to carry goods to the gold fields, and Helga walked carefully around each train, looking critically at the animals.

One mule driver, a medium-sized man with squinty little eyes, lank straw-colored hair, and a mean pinched face, gave Helga a dirty look and snarled at her as she looked at his team. "D'ya want me to pry open my mules' mouths, so you can look at their teeth, you old mud hen?"

Helga ignored him in a grand fashion. She walked away, went up to another driver, and pointed to us, our carpetbags, trunks, and provisions.

But the first driver would not be ignored. "What's the matter with my string?" he yelled at her. "My mules can carry more than any crowbait over there."

When Helga continued to ignore him, he turned to Mama and me, grinning evilly. "My handle's Arrowsmith Farr. I'll put your stuff on my team for ya, and I'll only charge two cents a pound for it."

Mama stiffened, but spoke up. "I was informed that the freight charge was a penny a pound."

Farr spat a wad of tobacco, which landed only a few inches from Mama's feet. "Blasted greenhorns are gettin' smarter all the time," he stated. "Better go back where you came from, lady. We don't need your kind up here. You just spoil the country."

Mama gasped and turned her back, but Jemmy reached into his back pocket and, in a flash, took out his slingshot. Before anyone could stop him, he picked up a stone, drew back the sling, and hit Arrowsmith Farr right on the nose with it.

Farr was so angry that he started for Jemmy, flourishing the long whip he used on his team and bellowing as he came. "I'll teach you, ya ornery brat, to get so free with that there peashooter."

Just before he reached us Helga appeared, and in

her hand was a tiny black gun, the smallest I had ever seen.

"Helga!" Mama exclaimed, pushing Jemmy behind her skirts.

"You just leave this rotten varmint to me, missus," Helga said in a hard voice.

"Now, lady, don't be hasty," the man said, showing his teeth.

"You git back to your mules," Helga ordered, "and don't you dare come near this lady or her children. That's an order, mister."

Farr smiled, made Helga a low mock bow that was somehow the nastiest thing he could have done, and swaggered back to his train, flicking his whip in an ugly fashion. We watched in helpless horror as he went up and down his train of mules whipping them cruelly. It was more than I could bear to see. When Farr reached the end of his train, he stood beside the smallest beast of all, a small gray animal with unhealed scars from former beatings, and whipped him harder than all the rest.

This was too much for Jemmy, who leaped forward like David attacking Goliath and fitted a second stone into his slingshot.

"Jemmy, come back here!" Mama called, looking more frightened than ever.

But the other steamer passengers had had enough of Farr's brutality, too, and a very tall man with a red mustache and a gray hat walked up to the driver and took the whip away as if it was nothing at all.

"That'll do!" was all the tall man said. "There ain't no sense in beating them mules, mister. They didn't do anythin'."

"They're my train," Farr said, snarling once again. "I'll beat 'em any time I take the notion."

"Not that little one!" Jemmy cried defiantly, standing in front of Farr with his slingshot in position.

"Oh, that old mule on the end?" Farr said, laughing. "He ain't worth much as a pack critter. He needs beatin' more'n all the others put together. There ain't no more stubborn mule in all Idaho Territory."

"Don't you dare hit him again!" cried Jemmy.

"Look, sonny, I'll do what I please with the cantankerous brute. Now you git out of my way," said Farr, as ugly a look on his face as I had ever seen.

"If you beat that mule, I'll hit you with this rock!"

"Tell you what, kid. I'll let you buy this here mule. How's that?"

"Mama, Mama!" Jemmy cried. "Did you hear that? The mule's for sale!"

"Oh, Jemmy," Mama said, "we don't need a mule."

"But he'll beat him to death—I know he will!" Jemmy wailed, beginning to create the sort of scene he knew Mama hated.

Mama looked around desperately. We had drawn quite a crowd of onlookers. "What shall I do, Miss Storkersen?" Mama appealed to Helga.

Helga pursed her lips and eyed the mule. Then she walked over to the animal, shoving Farr aside with her elbow. She opened the mule's mouth, felt his hide and ribs, looked at his eyes, and lifted each hoof in turn. Finally she came back to us.

"I side with sonny," she said quietly. "Buy the critter, missus. He can pull a purty good load if he's fed up a bit and given some good care. He ain't as old as he looks either. He can lug some of our stuff into the mines for us. That way we won't have to pay so much freight. We'll have to put your trunks on the other mules, though. There's no getting around that."

"A mule!" Mama wailed. "I didn't expect to have to buy a mule. What do they cost?"

"I'll find out; you won't be gypped," said Helga grimly, going over to Farr.

So there we stood for fifteen minutes, Jemmy nervously stomping up and down while Helga and Arrowsmith Farr bargained, both of them walking around and around the little mule, which Farr had cut out of the train.

At last Helga came back, shaking her head. "That mule skinner Farr is sure an ornery, mean cuss," she said. "He won't let us have the critter for a penny less than fifty dollars."

"Fifty dollars!" Mama cried out. "That's an outrage. The animal isn't worth that much money."

Helga shrugged. "It's the best I could do, missus. No horse trader could have done any better, and it's not so bad really. The mule'll pack your stuff in to Eagle City, and it'll come in real handy up there in the gold fields."

"Very well, Miss Storkersen," Mama said. "I give in against my better judgment. You pay that brute of a man." She took fifty dollars in greenbacks from her reticule.

However, Helga stood looking a moment at the greenbacks, sighing. "Mrs.," she said, "I know'd there was somethin' else I wanted to have us do at Fort Sherman. You should have had this here paper turned into gold or silver. They like hard money up here. They don't think paper money is just right somehow. I hope that Farr feller'll take it."

But after many scowls and what from a distance looked like very hard words, Farr did take the money, and Helga led the mule back to where we waited.

"Well, here he is, missus!" Helga announced. "He come along with me just like a lamb."

"Jemmy," Mama stated, "this is your animal. You care for him from now on."

33

"You do that, sonny," Helga said, "but, first of all, we pack our grub and light carpetbags on him. I'll put the trunks on them other mules over there. Then you got to manage him. Mules are just about the smartest critters there are. You got to treat them just right, so's they'll do things for you. But first, as I said, we got to get him all loaded."

And that's just what Helga did, as fast as you please, and with never a misstep. Then, to Mama's fright, she went to get the riding horses she had hired for us to ride to the gold fields.

When Helga returned she had three horses, two of them with sidesaddles. "It was a lucky thing to find these sidesaddles," she said. "You can ride behind me, little lady, or behind your maw."

"I can't do that!" said I in horror. "You can't expect me to ride astride and show my petticoats. I'm nearly fourteen!"

"Fiddlesticks!" Mama snapped, looking at her horse, a wall-eyed, ugly–looking yellow beast. "Climb up behind Miss Storkersen at once. I haven't ridden a horse in ten years, and I don't like the gleam in this animal's eyes. I can't fret about your petticoats right now, Ann Katherine."

So while a miner gallantly helped Mama onto her side-stepping, dancing horse and Jemmy dragged himself onto his little roan as if he did this every day, Helga and I found ourselves a low cut-off stump that

34

was the right height, and climbed onto an old fat bay mare. I held Helga around her not-so-small middle, and we set off for Eagle City at a trot, passing Arrowsmith Farr, who was packing his mule train to leave, too. He grinned at all of us, and I stuck my nose up into the air as high as I could. But at that moment Mama's yellow horse tried to bite Helga's mare, and it was all I could do to keep from sliding off over the tail, the mare bucked so much. My attempt to sniff haughtily at Arrowsmith Farr didn't come off so well.

I didn't find the going pleasant, hanging on for dear life behind Helga Storkersen. I most certainly was too nervous to notice much about the scenery, except that the pine-clad hills seemed to get steeper all the time and that we traveled mostly along trails at the bottom of canyons. We constantly kept crossing little streams that were very clear and looked very cold, judging from the patches of the snow along the banks, and I had the worst feeling that Helga's mare would decide to dump me off right in the middle of one of them.

Now and then when the going was a little easier, I looked back to see how Jemmy and Mama were doing. Mama had her hands full with her skittish yellow horse, but Jemmy was all right and still pulling his newly acquired mule, which, I must say, did seem to have decided to cooperate. Behind them plodded another mule train and behind those mules came Arrowsmith Farr and his string.

We rode for several hours and finally came out into an open space, ringed around with tall dark-green pines, where there were a few tents and a building which was certainly a saloon, judging by the tinkly piano music coming from it.

"This here's Evolution, ma'am," I heard a man say to Mama, as he trotted his horse up alongside hers and reined up.

"Humpf!" Mama sniffed. "It isn't much of a place, is it?"

"No, ma'am, it ain't. Everybody's gone to Eagle. You going to go inside for a while for some refreshment? We're going to stop here to rest the hosses."

"In a saloon. Mercy, no!" Mama cried out, shocked to the marrow of her bones.

"You don't have to have a lightnin' flash, ma'am."

"Whatever in the world is that?" Mama asked, as I strained to hear their conversation.

"A lightnin' flash is the same thing as a gum tickler. It's whisky, ma'am."

"Well, the names are certainly novel, but it's still the same disgusting stuff," said Mama.

"I'll bring you and your young'uns some sarsaparilla. By the way, my name's Luke Gordon."

Then the man, a large fellow with a brown mustache, a dark-blue neckerchief, and shiny black boots, lifted Mama down from her horse as if she was light as a feather.

"Would you help my daughter, please?" asked Mama, blushing.

The man bowed to her, came over, swung me down, and then held out his arms a little dubiously toward Helga. But Helga scorned him and unhooked herself from her sidesaddle, sliding to the ground.

Luke Gordon headed for the saloon while Helga and I made our way over to the log where Mama and Jemmy sat. After tying our horse's reins to a rickety hitching post, we sat on the log in front of one of the tents.

Jemmy, however, kept a firm hold on his mule's rope. "I don't want Timothy Clover to run away," he stated.

"Is that what you're going to call him?" I asked. "Don't you think that's a silly name?"

"Nope, it ain't silly. I like it."

"Jemmy," Mama warned, "your language is getting worse by the hour!"

We sat in tired silence for a time, until the nice man came back with four glasses of sarsaparilla, and joined us on the log to talk about his home in east Texas and how he had prospected all over the West. I noticed that he didn't drink any sarsaparilla, and I figured he'd had a lightnin' flash first.

At last we got up. We all thanked him for his

kindness, and mounted our horses once more, to travel up and down more canyons, to follow and cross more streams, although they probably were all the same winding one.

Helga chuckled to herself as we jogged along.

"What's funny, Helga?" I asked.

"I just bet your mama won't be a widow woman too long up here," she said. "She's still young and mighty purty, too."

"Mama remarry!" I said in wonder. "I just can't see her doing that."

"Eagle City'll be full of bachelors; one of 'em might even carry you off someday, little lady."

I turned the idea over in my head a few times. I must say that I favored it. I decided that I would set my cap for a tall, handsome, poetic boy with large melting brown eyes, if I ever found one suited to my taste.

"How about you, Helga?" I teased.

Helga sighed. "I'm a mud hen," she said. "That Arrowsmith Farr was right. I'm just an old fat Swede."

"But how about the fellow you had up here at the mines?"

"Oh, him? He used 'ter come around and jaw with me and sample my cookin', but he married a little bitty girl back in the Palouse country," she said. "That's when I decided to come up here."

"Oh," said I, disturbed at the tragedy of Helga's life. "But you'll find another fellow."

"The Lord be willin'," she said, sighing.

We traveled on after that without saying much else until we reached Eagle City. There it was, busy as a beehive, far busier than either Spokane Falls or Fort Sherman. The streets were alive with men, and everywhere houses and tents were going up. There was a sawmill running full blast down by the creeks, to supply timber for all this building. As we rode up the main street I counted two restaurants and three saloons, and read the shingles of some five doctors and even more lawyers. There was even a tent that bore the sign *The Eagle City Nugget*, and I figured correctly that this was the town newspaper. Then I spotted a sign, saying *Real Estate Agent.*

"Look, Mama!" I called out, pointing to it.

"I see it," Mama called back, over all the hammering and pounding, while her horse danced and shied at the noise.

We got off our horses by getting over against the wooden boardwalk and climbing off, and Mama thanked Luke Gordon and another man, called Montana, who had been kind to us on our journey from Cataldo Flats.

"If I can be of any help at all, ma'am, do call on me," said the man called Montana.

"Thank you," Mama said. "I'll do that. But where in the world would I ever find you?"

"My real name is Mortimer Bellows, and I own that building over there," he said, pointing across the street. "It ain't as fancy as Dutch Frank's, but it's the second biggest and best saloon in Eagle, and it's nothin' to be ashamed of. People all over Idaho Territory know about Montana Bellows' place."

"Oh," Mama said weakly, and Helga turned her back, so Mama couldn't see her laughing.

After the men left, Mama and I made our way to the real estate agent's office. A little bald man seated behind a desk made of two barrels and a plank looked up at us in surprise and then leaped to his feet.

"What can I do for you ladies?" he asked.

"Well, you can rent us one of your nicest furnished houses," Mama stated in her sweetest tones.

"A house!" he exclaimed. "Why, ma'am, there ain't a single house for rent anywheres in Eagle!"

"But that's impossible. I see houses going up all over the place."

"That's mostly business proppity, ma'am, or else they're all spoke for."

"Oh dear," said Mama. "Whatever shall we do?"

"But where do people sleep and eat in Eagle City?" I asked.

"They live in tents until they can build. Most of the prospectors don't want houses anyhow. They only come down out of the hills on Saturday and Sunday. Eagle's got a couple of eating houses, and you can get a plate of beans and a mug of coffee without too much trouble. We make out."

"But what shall we do?" Mama cried out. "We've come so far, and we're so tired. We've got to have some place to stay until school starts."

"School!" the man exclaimed. "There ain't no school in Eagle, ma'am. There ain't but three young'uns that age hereabouts anyhow."

"Well, there are five now," Mama said, leaning weak and pale against the wall. "I came here to teach the school. Whatever in the world can I do now?"

"If I was you, I'd go back where I came from," the man advised. "This ain't no place for widow ladies with young'uns."

"But I can't go back," Mama said.

"Well, in that case, ma'am, may I ask you a question?" the man asked. "Have you got your furniture and household stuff with you?"

"We have our household things," Mama said, "but no furniture."

"Well, you can make do for furniture, even if it'll be hard on nice ladies like you. As I see it, all you really need right now is a tent and a stove. I'll rent a tent to you, and you can buy a stove at one of the stores. I'd suggest a cookstove. One'll cost about a hundred dollars. Hope you got that much. I'll let

41

you have the tent and the land for twenty dollars a month, and I'm bein' generous, seein' as how you're new up here."

"All right," Mama said in the weakest voice I'd ever heard her use.

"I'll come over and show you how to put the tent up," said the man. "By the way, I'm Tom Webster."

Mr. Webster picked up his hat and opened the door for us, not bothering to lock his office, saying that there was nothing to steal in any event.

In deep silence we went back to where Helga and Jemmy waited, and after introducing Mr. Webster, Mama explained the situation. I could tell she didn't fancy the idea of living in a tent, and I agreed. Jemmy was thrilled, though, while Helga didn't even seem surprised.

We walked along the sidewalk to the edge of the town, rough-looking men staring at us at every step until Mr. Webster pointed to a bare spot on the street.

"This here's where you'll pitch your tent. It's near Pritchard Crick, so you can get water real easy. I'll go get the tent right away, and you better buy that there stove. It gets colder'n a hoot owl here at night, even though it is April. And, ma'am, if you ain't already got one, you'd better buy yourself a gun. There's no tellin' what kind of no-account varmint can come prowlin' around in the middle of the night."

"A gun!" said Mama, horrified. "I can't shoot a gun."

"I can!" Jemmy said with grim determination. "What kind of varmints, mister? Do you mean bears?"

"Nope, sonny," Mr. Webster said, shaking his head. "Bears scare off purty easy. I mean the two-legged kind of varmint. There's lots of them around these parts, and they can be a mite harder to deal with."

43

CHAPTER 4

Eagle City

"I'm not going to say a single solitary thing about prices any more. We're here, and we'll make the best of it. I suppose I can sell the stove again to someone else," said Mama through tight lips, as she and I hurried along to buy a cookstove. And Mama didn't say anything either when she paid out the hundred dollars for it instead of the twenty it would have cost in Portland.

The owner of the store took pity on us, I guess, for he cheerfully gave Mama gold coins for her greenbacks, saying that he was going to Spokane Falls soon and would exchange them there. He was even kind enough to have the cookstove sent over to the tent Mr. Webster was setting up for us, and it arrived there only minutes after we did.

We found Helga doing most of the work, while ordering the real estate agent about as if he had been a servant. She had the hammer lifted in both hands as we came up to her. "You hold that there stake jest as hard as you can," she was saying, "and I'll hit it a good crack with this here mallet of mine."

And she did too, right on the tent peg, while Mr. Webster looked nervous. It didn't take long for Helga to get the tent up and to shove, or "rassle" as she called it, the new stove inside.

"Let's hope this doesn't set fire to the tent," Mama commented, shaking her head.

"Well, we won't worry about it now; we'll try to make up a fire and get warm first," was Helga's comment in return.

While daylight remained Jemmy went out into the forest to cut evergreen boughs for mattresses, and Mama and I unpacked some of the things we'd need right away, such as pots and pans and our bedding. As for Helga, she was everywhere at once, sending Mr. Webster off for firewood and kerosene and buckets of water until we fled from her in terror.

In a short time we were as comfortable as we could be, given no furniture, with horsehair trunks for chairs and beds of green boughs. But we did have a good fire, and in no time at all our new cookstove glowed cherry red, giving out a wonderful warmth, which was needed in that cold April dusk.

"I'm awful hungry," Jemmy said. "That glass of sarsaparilla didn't hold me. We haven't had anything to eat since we left Fort Sherman."

"Sonny's sure right," Helga added. "I could use a good meal too, and I ain't had no time lately to cook any beans."

"We'll sample the food of Eagle City," Mama said, getting up and reaching for her bonnet. "But who'll watch the tent and our belongings?"

"That slipped my mind for sure," Helga replied, deep in thought, her face all screwed up with effort. "We better hire ourselves somebody."

Helga went out, and came back in a short time with a small shabbily dressed, red-haired man, who wore a fancy red mustache that curled up on both sides as nice as you please. He was wearing a black hat and smoking a black clay pipe, and we noticed that he wore a large black gun in a shiny leather holster on his hip.

"This here's O'Neil O'Neil—or that's who he claims to be," Helga announced. "He says he used ter be a miner. But he just ain't lucky, so he quit it for a while, and right now is down on his luck. He'll watch the tent and the mule for a dollar."

Mama flinched, but kept to her vow. Yet I knew how she felt—a dollar was a lot of money for something like that.

"Have no fear at all, madam," O'Neil O'Neil said in a high Irish voice, his blue eyes twinkling. "I'll take excellent care of everything. I'm an honest man despite the appearance I must make to your eyes. I fear that gold simply is not a metal that loves me, however. It flees from the stream beds when I approach the banks."

Mama looked at him a bit strangely, for I must admit he did talk differently from anyone I'd ever known, and he certainly looked as much like a desperado as most of the other men we'd seen on the streets of Eagle City.

"Just see to it that you do take care of things," Mama said. "We won't be gone long."

Off we went, bundled to the ears against the cold, and we stopped in front of one restaurant, which was a tent like ours, and looked at the copies of the bill of fare, tacked to the outside. Helga tore one off in the customary fashion before we went inside.

It certainly was the worst excuse I'd ever seen for a restaurant, but it was full. There were no tables at all—only long pine boards laid on sawhorses. There weren't any tablecloths or napkins, and only dirty-looking glass salt and pepper shakers. The tent had a dirt floor like ours, and I was sure it hadn't been swept for a month. Everywhere there were brass cuspidors.

"We got to eat somewhere, missus," said Helga, almost apologetically, as Mama stood there looking dismayed.

"I realize that, Miss Storkersen," replied Mama

with a sigh. "What do you suggest we eat? Something that's been boiled for hours I would think. I do have to protect the children's health."

"Let's set down then," Helga said, "but don't set at that table over there, unless you want to be within tobacco-spittin' distance of that Farr man."

I followed Helga's gaze, and, sure enough, there sat Arrowsmith Farr, pushing a piece of bread around on his plate to get the last bit of bean juice that remained. As I looked at him, he turned his head and grinned evilly.

Mama plunked us down at a table across the tent, and Helga handed her the bill of fare. "Beans with sowbelly, beans with bacon, beans with bear meat, just plain beans," Mama read aloud.

"Is that all?" Jemmy asked.

"That's all, sonny," Helga said. "This ain't Delmonico's. But there's coffee too."

Mama and I shuddered, but when the waiter, a dirty-handed, straggle-bearded old man arrived, Mama ordered coffee for herself and Helga and four plates of plain beans.

"You children will have to drink creek water until we can locate a cow," Mama said. "And to think they dare to charge two dollars a plate for beans!"

Our food came after a long wait, and when it finally did we wished it hadn't. The beans, which were served on tin plates and with tin spoons, were only half-cooked. I nearly broke a tooth on one and could not finish the plate.

Helga took one sip of her coffee, making a terrible face. "Ugh!" she said. "You could float an egg in this cup of poison."

"It is frightful, Miss Storkersen," Mama agreed, putting her mug down and looking a little green.

"Mrs.," Helga asked, leaning eagerly across the table, "why don't we open an eating house of our own? We can do a lot better'n this stuff here."

Mama sat for a long while, and then seemed almost to think aloud. "It's true this food is not fit for human beings," she said. "It's not even fit for pigs, I suspect. There aren't any children here to teach, and our money won't last forever—not the way I've been forced to spend it—so we do have to do something soon. But where would we go into business? There aren't any buildings available in Eagle City."

"We'll get us another and a bigger tent," Helga rushed on. "We'll have that sawmill do boards for us, jest like this here place. But we'll serve good, plain, well-cooked victuals from clean plates and for clean people. We'll even have tablecloths. I bet you got enough of 'em with you right now. We'll serve the best food in Eagle City. And no spittoons!"

Mama's cheeks were getting pinker by the minute as Helga talked, and I could tell that she liked the idea. "I think we should do it," she said. "We'll really do it! The best restaurant in Eagle City!"

"That's the ticket, Mama!" Jemmy cried.

"How about me, missus?" Helga asked. "Think you could see yer way clear to hire me now?"

"You're hired any time you want to be, Helga," Mama answered. "But I think that inasmuch as it was your idea and you'll be doing much of the work, you should be a full partner. I supply the money and table furnishings, and you supply the knowledge. How about that?"

Helga beamed happily, and Jemmy cried out, "Scott and Storkersen—the best plate of beans and sowbelly in Eagle City!"

We were all talking at once as we walked back through the night to our tent, but I was uncomfortably aware of how the miners stared at us. Eagle City was even more lively at night than in the daytime. Everywhere you went you heard the sound of pianos playing popular tunes, and you saw men going in and out of the doors of the saloons and gambling dens. Once we were shocked to see one miner shoot at the feet of another, just missing the toe of his boot. Then he laughed as if it was all very funny.

"Oh, dear, I've come a long way since we left Portland," Mama said. "I would have fainted dead away if I'd ever seen such a thing there. Helga, do you think such men can ever be tamed?"

"Oh, sure. They'll be just little old lambs when they come to our place. We'll make fellers like that hang up their hardware, or else they don't eat our grub. And nobody'll spit tobacco when I'm within seein' distance, believe you me, missus," was Helga's reply.

Mama sighed as we walked on, all of us stepping around a man who had taken too many gum ticklers and who sat on the sidewalk singing to himself.

We were at the end of the board sidewalk by this time, and our tent was not far. We started to cross the street, but stopped in sudden alarm. Without warning, Arrowsmith Farr, skinning knife in hand, came shooting around the corner of our tent with Timothy Clover in hot pursuit. Jemmy's mule was wild with anger, his long teeth bared in a wicked way and his ears flat against his head. He was right at Farr's coattail, his rope and stake trailing out behind.

"Get him, Timothy!" Jemmy yelled. "Go get him!"

"He was going to rob us!" Mama cried.

Farr's hair was flying and his mouth was open in fright, as he and the mule streaked past us down the street. Helga, Jemmy, and I ran as fast as we could after them, leaving Mama standing helplessly in the middle of the street. Miners leaped out of the way, grabbing for the sidewalk. Men came pouring out of saloons to see the fun, and stood there, slapping their knees with laughter and calling out encouragement to the mule and to Helga, Jemmy, and me.

The chase went on until Farr dove headfirst into a clump of bushes in the darkness at the other end of the street. This brought Timothy Clover to a skidding stop, and Jemmy was finally able to grab his rope. By the time Helga and I came up to them Jemmy had the mule calmed down.

"Timothy Clover didn't get him," Jemmy said sadly.

"Helga, was Farr going to kill him with that knife?" I asked.

"Nope, he'd of shot the critter if he wanted to kill him. He was goin' to slit the canvas of our tent and steal your maw's stuff."

As we plodded back up the street, our procession was cheered by a few miners, but we reached our tent without any further adventures. Mama was standing alone just where we'd left her in the middle of the street.

"Thank God!" she cried, when she saw us coming. "You're all right."

"Sure. Old Timothy Clover looks out for us," Jemmy boasted. "Aren't you glad now you bought him? He's better than any old watchdog."

"Well, he is quite an unusual mule," was as far as

Mama was willing to go. "But where is that O'Neil man?"

"There's only one way to find out," remarked Helga, untying a tent flap and going inside.

We went in after her, and I turned up the button of the kerosene lantern, which flickered blue and low, and cast frightening shadows on the tent walls. There lay O'Neil O'Neil snoring quietly, his head cradled on one of our carpetbags.

"How much was I to pay this worthless creature?" Mama asked Helga in scorn.

"Well, he sure ain't worth no dollar," Jemmy broke in.

Helga picked up Mama's parasol, which was lying alongside the carpetbag, and gave the man a sharp poke in the ribs. "You git up, you no-good loafer," Helga said fiercely. "Is this the way you take care of our stuff?"

O'Neil O'Neil opened his eyes and stared up at her. "Yes, dear lady?"

Helga brandished the parasol like a sword. "Don't 'dear lady' me. I sure ain't your 'dear' anything."

O'Neil O'Neil wore a look of great innocence as he got to his feet. "I appeal to you, madam," he said to Mama. "Can you control this vision of Nordic loveliness, who seems determined to strike me with a parasol?"

Mama stared coldly at him a moment before she

54

spoke. "You were hired expressly to watch this tent and the goods in it."

"I have been faithful to my trust," O'Neil O'Neil protested. "Indeed, I have, madam."

"Well, it might interest you to learn that an attempt was made to rob this tent."

"You're just lucky that my mule was outside," cried Jemmy. "My mule chased the robber off."

"Is this tale true?" O'Neil inquired, looking at Helga, who had lowered the parasol.

"It sure is," Helga said. "We ought ter pay sonny's mule."

"But, dear lady, I was not sleeping—I was only meditating," O'Neil O'Neil protested.

"Well, meditate away from here!" Mama said angrily, giving him a silver dollar.

"Perhaps I can be of service to you and your charming family again," murmured O'Neil, taking the dollar and bowing grandly to Mama and Helga.

Mama did not reply but turned away as O'Neil left our tent.

Helga was standing holding the parasol to her chest, a dreamy smile on her lips. "What does Nordic mean?" she asked me.

"I think it means, Norwegian or Swedish," I said.

"What does meditating mean, little lady?" she asked, staring at the tent wall, her eyes round and shiny in the lantern light.

"Thinking," I replied.

"Ain't it a beautiful word, though?" Helga breathed. "He talks so fine that I can hardly understand him."

"Fiddlesticks!" Mama exploded. "He would have let that Farr person steal everything we owned. How can you say anything good at all about him?"

"I think we ought to take him on to help out when we start our eatin' house," said Helga.

But Mama shook her head and looked sharply at her. "No, we will not have him around here. We'll have nothing to do with dreamy, romantic loafers."

Helga put down the parasol almost as if she hadn't heard Mama; she acted as if she was having a beautiful dream. I looked at Jemmy and winked. For once I was going to bet against Mama. If Helga wanted O'Neil O'Neil around, he'd be around.

Oh, how we worked the next few days. I don't know when I have ever been so busy.

Helga and Mama went to see Mr. Webster, and they contracted for another and a larger tent, and then we all went to the sawmill and ordered long planks for our tables. While the planks were being fashioned, Mama and Helga bought a second and larger cookstove, for we could not do all the cooking we planned on one stove.

Jemmy cut wood and chopped kindling until he

56

had a huge pile of it out behind the large tent, but finally he got so tired that Mama gave in to Helga's pleas and hired O'Neil O'Neil to take care of our wood for the two stoves.

It was a good thing, too, for O'Neil O'Neil was a clever carpenter and made some rough furniture for us, including the sawhorses for the restaurant tables.

As for me I went through our horsehair trunks and took out everything I thought we would need. We had plenty of tablecloths and napkins and the like, but not enough silver or plates. So we had to buy tin plates and tin utensils, which I knew Mama hated for their roughness and cheap looks.

At the store Mama bought more flour, beans, corn meal, bacon, and a cask of dried apples. She sighed silently at the prices.

"You can pass the word around, if you'll be so kind, that we shall be opening a restaurant in three days," Mama told the store owner.

"Now that's real good news," said the man. "I'll come eat at your place myself, although sowbelly and beans are pretty much the same everywhere you go."

"They'll be different at our place," I spoke up, coming up to the counter with three small onions in my hand.

"That'll be a dollar, little girl," the man said, making me angry by calling me "little girl."

57

"A dollar for three onions!" Mama cried, shocked once more.

"Yep," said the man. "They're as scarce as hen's teeth up here. People eat 'em raw like apples."

Mama shuddered and turned to Helga. "Miss Storkersen, it's high time we planted those seeds you bought in Fort Sherman. Do you suppose you could get Mr. O'Neil to clear a patch of ground in back of our tent?"

Helga nodded happily and blushed. "Sure, missus. He'd do just about anything I asked him to do, you betcha."

"Well then," Mama went on, "we'll get a garden in, and we'd better send him out hunting. We're serving more than beans in our restaurant."

On Helga's orders O'Neil O'Neil left at noon the next day to bring back some bear fat. Our prime need was the lard for the bread and pies she planned to bake, so she told him not to bother about any meat. There was time for that later.

Jemmy was quite upset, because he had not been permitted to go with O'Neil O'Neil, but he became more cheerful when Mama promised to buy him a fishing line and fish hooks, and told him that she would count on him to keep the restaurant supplied with trout and whitefish.

I was worried, though. I knew how little money

was left, for I had peeked into Mama's old pocketbook and had seen that very few gold eagles still lay there. If the restaurant didn't succeed, I didn't know what we would do. We wouldn't have enough to get back to Portland and set up a house again. The only thing we could do would be to go to work for someone else right here in Eagle City or perhaps in Spokane Falls, and nobody would take all of us Scotts together. I'd have to go out as a hired girl and break up the family, and that would probably mean that I would never go to school again. Jemmy said that he didn't care about school, but I did. I liked it.

I must have looked as sad as I felt, because Helga laughed at me. "Come on, smile, little lady," she said. "It ain't as bad as all that. Come see what I'm doin'."

"What's that for, Helga?" I asked, without much interest as she poured hot water into a bowl over a mixture of flour and salt. "We aren't opening for two days yet."

"I'm makin' the starter for the sody biscuits and sour-dough bread," she explained. "I'm goin' to keep this here stuff until it gets sour and bubbles, and i'll hang on to some of it from now on. I ain't got the yeast I'd like ter have, and I don't know anybody to get some riser from. O'Neil says he ain't got any left."

"Oh," said I, becoming interested at last. We had bought our bread from a bakery in Portland, and I knew nothing much about baking.

"Sure," Helga went on, putting the bowl on the warm shelf above one of our kitchen stoves. "I'll make doughnuts and crullers from this too, when O'Neil gets back with bear lard. Then he'll go out again for a buck deer. We'll set quite a table here."

"What'll we serve, Helga?" I asked. I sat down at one of the benches O'Neil had made and looked around at our neat tent, with its packed-dirt floor and three rows of clean pine-board plank tables.

"Well," said Helga, staring at the roof of the tent while counting on her fingers, "we'll serve beans with bacon or sowbelly for them as wants it. We'll have venison liver, venison chops and steak, and venison stew with onions—that'll be the most expensive natcherly. We'll have apple pie and lots of good coffee. We'll have fried trout, if sonny catches any, and later on we'll be havin' venison mincemeat, huckleberry pies, elderberry jelly, huckleberry muffins, broiled squirrel, bear paws, beaver tail, and roast elk shoulder."

"Bear paws and beaver tail!" Mama exclaimed, coming up behind me so suddenly that I jumped.

"Sure, missus. Those are real good eatin'."

Mama shuddered at the thought, and I must say I did agree with her.

"What shall we charge, Helga?" Mama asked, bringing paper, pen, and the ink bottle to one of the tables, and seating herself with a rustle of her black skirts.

"We'll charge pretty much what the others do around here, missus. It'll be two dollars for a plate of beans and bacon, two-fifty for the venison liver, chops, and steak, and three dollars for the venison stew that has onions in it."

"That's very high, isn't it?" Mama asked, not having written down a word.

"No, it ain't," Helga stated flatly. "Pardon me for speakin' right out, missus, but you saw what it costs for grub up here. We got to charge that much to keep goin', not to speak of makin' a profit."

"But three dollars for stew!" Mama protested.

"It's more work than any of the other things, and it's got onions at thirty-three cents apiece, too," Helga said. "People get awful tired of beans all the time. You jest put down three dollars for that deer stew, missus. It'll go faster'n anythin' else. You jest wait and see now."

Mama smilingly dipped her pen into the ink and began to make up our menu as Helga dictated. Helga had won again. It was really amazing how she had taken over our lives in such a short time, especially after she had made such a bad impression on Mama on the coach from Rathdrum to Fort Sherman. I don't know what we Scotts would have done in Idaho Territory if it hadn't been for Helga Storkersen— probably have starved to death, or gone back to Portland like whipped dogs.

Our menu looked quite elegant, so elegant that Mama debated whether or not to take it over to the *Eagle City Nugget* tent and have some posters made up, but Helga said that wouldn't be necessary. "Don't you fret yourself, missus," she said. "The word'll be all over this here gold camp by tomorrow mornin' that two ladies is openin' a real fine eatin' place with home cookin'. O'Neil will make us a sign, and the little lady here can make up copies of what we're goin' to serve."

And that's just what I did for the next two days—I copied our menu over and over, while O'Neil O'Neil came and went, bringing in venison and bear fat. Helga and Mama got things ready, staying up to all hours, making apple pies, preparing biscuit dough, and stirring wonderful-smelling pots of beans and stew in great copper washtubs on our two gleaming cookstoves.

Scott and Storkersen's Restaurant, the Finest in Eagle City, was due to open at noon the next day, and I went to bed the night before with a bad case of writer's cramp and a worse case of the worries. Jemmy and Helga slept as if they didn't have a single care in the world, but I saw that Mama tossed and turned sleeplessly.

I knew what she was thinking, for I was thinking the same thing. Would anyone come tomorrow?

CHAPTER 5

Scott and Storkersen

As it turned out, I had nothing much to worry about. Scott and Storkersen opened promptly at noon, with an army of hungry men descending on us. Everyone we knew in Eagle City was standing outside waiting when Mama went out to untie the tent flap. There they were—Montana Bellows, Mr. Webster, Luke Gordon, all the storekeepers, and many more besides, all with their hats off, and dressed in the best clothes they had. I never saw so many flowered and checked vests and such heavy gold watch chains before in my life, not to mention well-brushed beards and waxed mustaches.

I think that if Mama had been a man they might have trampled her in the mud to get a seat at one of our tables, but because she was Mama, they all bowed low as they trooped past her and into the tent.

They got quite a surprise there, though, because O'Neil O'Neil sat behind a table looking quite fierce, and as each man went by, he recited, as if by memory, "If you will be so kind as to let me have your pistols, six guns, derringers, bowie knives, and whatever else you have in the line of weapons and armament, I will hold them for you, as well as hold your hats. There are, as you will note, no cuspidors in this fine establishment, and there will consequently be no chewing of tobacco permitted. There will be no smoking of any sort and no rough language, and no one will put his feet on the table, as in other cafés I can name."

Some of the men grumbled, but most of them laughed, and all did as O'Neil requested. In a little while I caught a hurried glimpse of his table out of the corner of my eye, and saw that it was piled high with hats and various types of guns.

I say I only caught a quick glimpse, because, of course, Mama, Jemmy, and I were the waiters, while Helga stood by the stoves, putting the food on the tin plates. It wasn't very hard. After all, our menu wasn't long, and I didn't have to write down fancy orders as they do in regular restaurants. Helga was right too—venison stew was the most popular dish. I positively flew back and forth, carrying plates of the wonderful-smelling stew, topped with Helga's light-as-a-cloud sody biscuits. It wasn't long before we were out of it. And it surely was a good thing that Helga and Mama had baked several dozen apple pies, for almost every man there ate two pieces of them. And how the men could drink coffee! They must have drunk gallons of it.

"Best cup of coffee I've had since I left San Francisco," Luke Gordon said to Montana Bellows and me, as I brought him his fourth cup.

"I'm glad you like it, Mr. Gordon," I said politely.

"You folks got yourselves a real success here," Montana said, jabbing his fork into a piece of apple pie. "You'll do a sight better here than the miners will do. There ain't many who strike it rich at the diggin's, but nobody starves who's got a business that does the supplyin' for them that gambles."

O'Neil O'Neil was taking in silver dollars as fast as he could, as the miners and the townsmen came up to his table. It was unusual to have someone take the money this way. But Mama thought it would be better for O'Neil to do it. This wasn't Portland, so O'Neil had our shotgun right alongside his chair in case anyone didn't behave like a gentleman. We had worried a bit about this arrangement, fearing that our customers wouldn't like it, but it seemed there was nothing at all to fret about.

"It's a success; our place is a real success!" I crowed to Helga, who stood at the stove ladling up a plate of beans and bacon.

"Sure, what'd I tell you?" was Helga's comment.

"It's even more of one than you think. Did you see who jest came in? We've been honored with Eagle City's leadin' citizen."

"Where?" asked I.

Helga gave me the plate, and nodded toward a corner of our tent, where a brown-bearded, plainly dressed man sat alone. "That there's Mister Andrew Pritchard," she said. "You jest take him this plate of beans and sody biscuits."

I did as Helga said, threading my way carefully among our tables, and set the hot plate down in front of Mr. Pritchard, the man who had found the first gold in the Coeur d'Alenes. He did not speak at all, but he did smile at me for a second, and then picked up his fork, not his spoon, and went to work on his beans. I saw that his table manners were quite as good as my own, and considerably better than Jemmy's were at the moment. I could well believe what people said about Mr. Pritchard's being a gentleman.

On my way back to the stoves with some empty plates I couldn't help but see that Dutch Frank, too, had come to dine at Scott and Storkersen's on Helga's venison steak. There he sat, the owner of Eagle's biggest saloon, biting into a biscuit and nodding to himself in a very contented and satisfied way.

As usual, Helga was right. We were a success of the first order.

* * *

A month went by, and we were so busy with our eating establishment that we didn't even know the time had passed, until O'Neil O'Neil came up to Mama one afternoon after our diners had left. He stood before her, his old black hat held against his chest, and there was a troubled look on his usually merry face. "Madam," he said, "I do not mean in any way to give the impression that I am dissatisfied with the conditions of my employment here, but, alas and alack, the truth of the matter is that I feel a call."

"A call? What kind of call would that be, Mr. O'Neil?" Mama said, frowning a little. She had never quite forgiven him for going to sleep the night Arrowsmith Farr tried to rob us, and she didn't take kindly to conversations with him.

"I feel I must commune once more with the elements," O'Neil answered. "Now that summer is upon us, I have a wish to go out into the mountains once more, and seek for the precious stuff that lies there eluding me."

"Oh, that. You mean you want to go prospecting again?"

"Precisely."

"Really, Mr. O'Neil," Mama said crossly, "why couldn't you come right out with it? You know we need you here."

"Oh, let him skedaddle, missus," Helga called, up to her elbows in bread dough at one of the tables. "Let him git pine cones in his whiskers if he wants to."

"I don't approve of this behavior," Mama stated. "But I can't hold you here, Mr. O'Neil. I shall pay you your remaining wages, and I shall try to find a replacement for you at once."

O'Neil broke into a grin. "That will not be necessary, madam. I have considered the problem carefully, and consequently have secured someone to take up my duties."

"Well, that sure takes nerve," Helga said admiringly. "Where is this here replacement of yours?"

"I shall bring him to meet you at once, ladies," stated O'Neil, who bowed and left the tent.

"Don't he beat all, though?" Helga asked. "I never knowed a man like that there O'Neil O'Neil. No wonder his maw named him the same thing twice over."

Mama bit her lip, and went over to a metal chest we kept, unlocked it, and took out some silver dollars. There was a bank in Eagle City, but it was in a tent too, and Mama felt that if a bank wasn't a brick or marble building, it wasn't safe, so we kept our cash in our own strongbox.

O'Neil returned in a quarter of an hour, followed by a tall, dark-skinned, sad-looking man, dressed in buckskin trousers. Long black braids fell over his shoulders from under his high-crowned black hat, and bright-yellow garters supporters held up the sleeves of his red calico shirt.

"Allow me to present my friend and compatriot, Nehemiah Spotted Horse. He chops wood, sweeps out tents, carries water, and does everything else necessary to the performance of my former duties," said O'Neil.

Mama sank down on a bench staring at O'Neil O'Neil and his replacement, while Helga came around and stood beside her, white flour-covered hands on her hips.

"O'Neil O'Neil!" Helga boomed. "Have you lost what sense you ever did have to begin with?"

"I am in perfect possession of my not inconsiderable faculties," O'Neil protested. "This gentleman here has accompanied me on various prospecting expeditions heretofore, but this time I have decided that he needs the social polish that only two ladies of culture and breeding can give him. He is informed of what will be expected of him."

"Can he take in the cash and make the change?" Helga asked.

"That, alas, he cannot do," O'Neil admitted. "However, he knows the herbs and fruits of the area as no one else does. You say you have longed for salads and greens, dear ladies—here is your menu brightener! He also hunts superbly, and you do not need anyone to take the money at the door. You are an old and established firm, as Eagle City business goes. No one will attempt to defraud you by departing before he has paid. If he attempted such a deed, one of your many friends would riddle him with bullets, if not do something less civilized."

Mama looked at Nehemiah Spotted Horse and shook her head. "Where in the world would he stay?" she asked.

"He has already pitched his tepee down close to the creek's edge," said O'Neil. "He is ready to go to work."

And at these words Nehemiah grabbed a broom that was leaning against the tent wall, and vigorously began to sweep the floor.

"Oh, no!" Helga cried out. "Stop him, O'Neil. He'll get dirt and dust all over the bread dough."

O'Neil spoke to him sharply in some language I'd never heard before, and the Indian put down the broom and removed his hat.

"Great heavens, doesn't he speak English?" asked Mama.

"Sad to say, he is not fluent," O'Neil replied. "I addressed him just now in Chinook, the tongue universally used by the Indians west of the Rocky Mountains. He comprehends nearly everything said to him in English, however."

"Oh, dear, the things I've done since I came up into these wilds," she said. "I do desperately need someone to help us out. Shall we hire the man, Helga?"

"Ah sure," said Helga, "he handles a broom real good."

"Well," Mama said, "just to be certain, I think I'll go over and call on Mr. Gordon to see what he thinks of this."

Mama threw a shawl over her shoulders, tied on her bonnet, and left hurriedly.

"Well," said Helga, "I got to get back to the bread. I just hope you don't stick your fingers in the risin' dough, Spotted Horse. I don't put up with that."

Nehemiah grinned and shook his head. "Me know better."

Helga laughingly said, "We'll git along then," and walked back to her baking pans.

O'Neil O'Neil didn't follow her as usual, but wandered over to me, leaving Nehemiah standing with his arms folded in the middle of the tent. "Did you ever entertain the idea of prospecting yourself, little lady?" he asked me.

"Sure," I responded. "But Mama won't let me go up into the hills, and she won't let Jemmy go either. She says it's too dangerous and that there are bears and mountain lions all over the place."

"That is true. Your mother is a wise woman," said O'Neil.

"I think she really means the two-legged varmints," I added, amazing myself at the words I now used so easily, for I would never have said *legs* to anyone before. I would have said *limbs*, and would have felt very daring about that.

O'Neil seated himself beside me and went on. "But have you no desire at all to seek gold?"

"Oh, yes," I replied truthfully. "I'd love to, but it seems that I just can't."

"Your brother is going along with me," O'Neil said quietly.

"He is!" I cried, angry at the idea that Jemmy was going. Boys got to do everything they wanted to do one way or another, just because they were boys.

"Well, in a sense he is," O'Neil explained. "He is a partner in my enterprise. He is grubstaking me."

"What with?" I demanded, for I knew all about grubstaking. It meant simply that you helped outfit a prospector, and if he found anything, part of that gold belonged to you. I knew very well, too, that Jemmy spent every penny Mama gave him on candy at the stores. He couldn't resist horehound candy, and he couldn't possibly have any money. He never did.

"He's lending his mule to me as a pack beast. I believe he refers to the creature as Timothy Clover."

"I've earned five silver dollars from tips," I said. "If Jemmy can put in fifty dollars' worth of mule, I can put in five dollars' worth of silver. Will you take it, and let me be a partner, too?"

"This I shall do," said O'Neil O'Neil. "And in a way then, you shall also go prospecting with me. Your silver will return to you many times over."

"Don't tell Mama," I warned in a whisper, "and better not tell Helga either."

"Miss Storkersen, that jewel of a woman, has already joined my venture as a partner," said O'Neil. "I shall miss her wonderful meals and her sprightly conversation, but it will be beans her money has purchased that will feed me in the wilderness."

"Where did the money you earned here go?" I asked him.

"Here and there," he said, shrugging his shoulders. "Hither, thither, and yon."

I nodded, for I suspected that it went for gum ticklers and lightnin' flashes, having seen O'Neil head for Dutch Frank's often enough after we closed in the evening. However, I was now his partner, so I said nothing.

Mama came back in a few minutes, and while she untied her bonnet strings she addressed O'Neil. "Mr. O'Neil, it seems that Nehemiah has a good enough reputation. Consequently, I shall hire him on your recommendation but will, of course, pay him three quarters of your salary, because he will not act as cashier for us. Mr. Gordon has suggested this arrangement. Do you think that will be fair?"

Once more O'Neil spoke to the Indian in Chinook, and Nehemiah Spotted Horse beamed and nodded.

"All right," Mama said, "but I'll hold you responsible."

"Fear not, dear lady," said O'Neil. "I shall depart at the crack of dawn, when fair Aurora first appears. Nehemiah Spotted Horse will begin to fill the wood box at that precise moment."

Well, thought I, I'll have to get up early, too, and give O'Neil my five dollars then. I couldn't do it now with Mama looking right at me, and besides, I wanted to wish O'Neil good luck. I knew that I wouldn't have to wake Jemmy. He'd be there to take a tender farewell of his beloved Timothy Clover.

Mama was furious next day when she learned that Jemmy had sent Timothy Clover off with O'Neil O'Neil without saying a word to her about it. She boxed his ears and ordered him to bed without any supper. Jemmy knew that I had grubstaked O'Neil too, but he didn't tattle to Mama, which was very noble of him. I must say, though, that I did feel quite guilty about it all. I felt I should tell Mama and take my punishment, but I just couldn't find the right words, although I tried hard enough in the next few weeks after O'Neil left.

I don't know if Mama would really have heard me anyway, for she was so busy supervising Nehemiah Spotted Horse that she was almost beside herself. He had to have everything demonstrated to him, motion by motion, but he only had to be shown a thing once, and always after that did it perfectly.

Nehemiah spoke little, but had the largest vocabulary of grunts I had ever heard. He could say more that way than Jemmy could in the English language. He was a better fisherman than Jemmy too, and could be counted on to come back every day with a mess of trout or whitefish, so fried fish became a regular part of our bill of fare. Nehemiah always returned from the hills and canyons with wild gooseberry and currant shoots, which Mama made us eat, for she feared scurvy and would watch us carefully to see that we weren't developing it. Nehemiah also showed Jemmy and me where to pick salal berries, which made good pies, and showed us where the huckleberries and elderberries were ripening. Helga said that huckleberries made the best pies and muffins you ever tasted and that elderberry jelly was the finest there was.

Our bill of fare was really growing; ours was the most popular restaurant in Eagle City. Our garden was nearly up now, so we would soon have all kinds of vegetables. And the men who ate regularly at our place brought us things from Spokane Falls and Fort

Coeur d'Alene—or rather they brought them to Mama, for it looked as if half of the gold camp was sweet on her. Montana Bellows brought her a rhubarb plant and a rose bush from Spokane Falls, and I think Mama was as pleased over the rose bush as she was over the rhubarb. Dutch Frank left a little lilac tree in front of our tent one morning, and Andrew Pritchard once brought us a brace of ducks he had shot, which Helga promptly roasted, dispatching one to Mr. Pritchard with Jemmy as delivery boy.

The best gift of all, to my mind, though, came from Luke Gordon, who rode up one day with two wooden crates, one on either side of his horse. Such a loud cackling sounded from those crates that Mama and Helga dashed out into the street, with their aprons still on and without their bonnets.

"Chickens!" Mama exclaimed. "Real honest-to-goodness chickens!"

Mr. Gordon took off his hat and smiled. "I brought six hens and one rooster from the Fort, Mrs. Scott. Please take 'em off my hands. The birds are drivin' me crazy with all the noise they make."

Helga was speechless; her eyes bulged. "Eggs!" she said finally. "Real eggs for a real breakfast. Flapjacks! No hide or hair or feathers of those chickens will be put in a stew pot here. Real eggs! Do you suppose, missus, that Nehemiah can build us a chicken coop?"

"If he can't, I can," said Jemmy, who had come out of the tent behind us.

And Jemmy was true to his word. Nehemiah Spotted Horse made it clear right away that he wasn't a carpenter, so Jemmy made a fine, tight, varmint-proof chicken coop. Mama had to buy grain for the chickens from Fort Sherman, for we had the only chickens in Eagle City, it seemed. But she didn't mind—it was so good to have eggs again now and then—even if we did have only six hens and couldn't have omelets every day of the week. It did mean one thing, though. Helga had to move her bed over to the back of the tent as close to the chicken coop as she could get, and she kept our shotgun right by her side, for she swore that no Eagle City loafer was going to run off with one of our birds if she had anything to say about it.

We didn't have a lot of time to tease Mama about all of her admirers and the gifts they brought her, for we kept open every day but Monday. We had thought of closing Sundays, but Mama said she just couldn't do it. The thought of those hungry men eating Sunday dinner at the bad restaurants of Eagle City bothered her a great deal. She set great store on Sunday dinner, and that day we served our very best.

Just writing up our Sunday bills of fare made me hungry. We had broiled squirrel, venison stew, pheasant with gravy and diced salt pork, elk steak, venison mincemeat pies made with a bear lard crust, apple grunt, trout dipped in melted lard and corn meal and fried golden brown. Mama refused to serve beans on Sunday. She said that as long as there was no church in Eagle City, we would try to keep one part of the Sabbath the way we always did in Portland, by having a real good Sunday dinner, and that did not mean beans in any form.

Mama always made us say grace before we had our Sabbath meal, and I noticed that some of the men said it silently too. Nor did we ever charge for the coffee that came with that dinner. Helga said if anybody ever tried to pay her for a second cup of coffee on Sunday, she'd throw it all over him, and Mama felt it wouldn't be Christian to make them pay. So it seemed to me that all I ever did on Sunday was to wander around the tables holding our big graniteware coffee pot with a pot holder, pouring out cup after cup of Helga's hot, strong, good-smelling coffee.

Our customers were very nice men in most cases. Now and then Helga had to tell one to take his feet off the table or to watch his language, but they always obeyed her. We never had anyone come in who had taken too many gum ticklers, and Helga said that Dutch Frank and Montana Bellows must be keeping men like that away from our place, since they knew how Mama felt about such things.

Jemmy informed me, though, that we had some

real desperadoes eating at our restaurant every single night. One of them, who seemed to me to be the most quiet and gentlemanly customer of all, outside of Mr. Pritchard, was a notorious gunman and killer. Jemmy said with awe that he was so fast with his gun that he would challenge another man to draw on him, deliberately drop his own gun on the floor, pick it up, and shoot before the second man could draw his six shooter from his holster and pull the trigger. I was not impressed, however, and Mama said it was revolting and barbarous. Anyway the desperado made no trouble, so we continued to serve him.

Then, of course, there were the painted ladies from the saloons and dance halls. I had thought "painted ladies" meant the little spiced crab apples that had their sides painted with currant jelly and were served with pork roast in Portland, but I learned better in Eagle City. These Idaho Territory painted ladies wore nodding plumes of ostrich feathers in their hair, red silk stockings, bright-colored satin dresses and short skirts, which showed under the dark cloaks they always wore to our place. Mama said that I was not to talk to them, so I didn't, and I must say that none of them ever attempted to talk to me. Helga sometimes called one or two of them by name, and said they were nice girls. But Mama only sniffed at this, and stated that as long as they behaved themselves and didn't get too friendly they were welcome enough.

She added, too, that any woman who wore paint was no lady, and that the only thing a real lady did was to rub a little red flannel on her lips to redden them, although even that should be kept a secret. Naturally I tried wetting some red flannel and rubbing it across my lips, but I couldn't see that it made them a bit pinker, so I gave it up.

Mama had changed a little since we had come to Eagle City, but not as much as Jemmy and I had. Jemmy had gone almost as wild as the eagles that nested in the tall trees up in the hills. His grammar was terrible. Mama couldn't do a single thing with him, and it worried her. She'd even given Helga permission to whale him if he needed it.

I had changed too. I didn't use such bad grammar as Jemmy did, but I used Eagle City expressions all the time. I called people from California "self-risers," because they used self-rising flour, and if anybody asked for a "jawbone," I knew he wanted his food on credit. I called a lantern a "palouser," and although Mama didn't know it, I knew that a "mid-air dance" meant a hanging. I even wished that we had come to Eagle City earlier so that I could have seen the famous Calamity Jane and her troupe of dancing girls, who had come over the snow-covered trails from Montana Territory in February of 1884—not of course, that Mama would have permitted me to see them.

* * *

Although several weeks passed, we did not hear a single word from O'Neil O'Neil. Jemmy was worried about Timothy Clover, and asked the prospectors about him when they came into our restaurant on their weekends down in Eagle City. But it seemed that no one at all had seen O'Neil or Jemmy's mule. Helga was also a little upset over not hearing from him, although she didn't say much. However, she didn't sing Swedish songs when she kneaded the bread dough the way she once did.

Nehemiah Spotted Horse didn't seem to worry, though. "He turn up," he said, stalking off to fill the wood box again.

But one warm Sunday afternoon we had news of another kind, and it was not welcome news either. Mr. Webster, the real estate agent, stopped Mama and Helga for a few moments when he came in for his dinner, and Jemmy and I overheard what he said. "I don't want to bother you ladies with bad tidin's," he stated, "but I thought you might want to know. That bad actor, Arrowsmith Farr, was seen at Cataldo Flats just the other day. I'd watch out for him if I was you folks. He's said all over camp that he's goin' to get you for makin' a fool of him the time your boy's mule chased him."

"Thank you for your warning, Mr. Webster," Mama said. "We shall keep a close watch."

"Did you buy a gun like I told you?" asked Mr. Webster, concerned.

"We sure did," Helga replied. "We'll load him up on buckshot, if he comes around here."

Jemmy had added nothing to this conversation, but only stood there frowning, uncomfortable in the starched, tight-collared Sunday shirt Mama had made him wear. "I'd sure feel a lot better about this news if we had old Timothy Clover here," he said finally. "He could sniff out that mean cuss, Farr, a whole mile away."

Mama put her arm around Jemmy for a moment. "I wish he was here too, Jemmy," she said softly. "I certainly do."

CHAPTER 6

Ann Katie's Wardrobe

So there we were—waiting for O'Neil O'Neil to come back out of the hills and for Arrowsmith Farr to do something desperate to us. It was very hard on our nerves. Every time anyone fired a shot or every time we heard a mule bray, Jemmy popped outside to see who it was and what was going on. But it was never either of them. Just the same, though, we kept on with our restaurant, and we couldn't complain about business.

We did very well indeed, particularly now that our vegetable garden was up. Mama put more and more gold eagles into our little locked box, but she seemed worried and tired. I knew she was upset over Arrowsmith Farr's being seen around, and I knew, too, that I slept lighter than usual as I listened and waited. Helga slept even closer to the back of the tent flap, and practically lay on our shotgun, but we were still uneasy.

Jemmy was sure that Farr wouldn't bother any of us; his chief worry was that he might somehow find Timothy Clover and harm him. Sometimes I believed that my brother thought more of that mule than he did of us. At least he acted as if he did.

Helga wasn't too happy. It was clear to me that she missed O'Neil. When someone came into the tent, she always looked up from whatever she was doing and then looked away just as quickly. Jemmy said that she was sweet on O'Neil O'Neil, but I found that hard to believe. She was nearly six inches taller than he was. And how could a lady be sweet on someone that much shorter?

Mama had more admirers than ever, although most of them didn't dare speak to her, because she was such a fine lady. But Luke Gordon and Montana Bellows talked to her every chance they got, and ate at our place three times a day. I think they would have liked to take her to church socials, but there still wasn't any church in Eagle City. So the only place they could have taken her was to a saloon or a dance hall, and Mama would have died first. I noticed that they were jealous of one another, too, because each glared when the other one talked alone to Mama. I thought it was all very romantic, but no one paid any attention to me, least of all Jemmy, who was wilder than ever.

I tried to make myself feel more cheerful by making our tent a nicer place to live. It was summer now, and I kept it filled with lilacs from the bush we'd been given and wild syringa from the hillsides. I saw to it that it was swept and dusted, and I certainly did wish that we could have green velvet curtains. But where could you put curtains in a tent? To tell the truth, I was very tired of living in it, and I longed to have a room of my own again. I was tired of taking my dresses out of carpetbags and heating Mama's sadirons on the stove, so I could iron them. Then as soon as they were ironed, I had to put them right back, folding them up and wrinkling them all over again. How I wished for a place to hang something up!

I was out by the campfires in back one morning stirring our two heavy copper washtubs with a wooden stick while our linen and clothing steamed and boiled, when Mama stepped out with a bucket of chicken feed. "You should put a little more soap in those kettles, Ann Katherine," she said critically. "Our Sunday tablecloths have to be just as white as we can get them. Now you do that while I feed the laying hens."

I put the stick into one kettle and pushed the heavy cloth around, which is a job I've always hated. "Mama," I said, "we need a wardrobe closet for our tent. It's too much work to iron each dress and apron twice."

Mama thought for a moment, and then nodded. "You are perfectly right, Ann Katherine. I've thought of it myself. We can afford it, and we'll find a use for it when we go back home. Why don't you go to the sawmill and ask about a carpenter? We'll have a wardrobe built, and it will be your responsibility."

"It'll have to be big," I explained, "big enough to hold all of our things and Helga's, too."

"Certainly," Mama agreed. "When you finish there, just go on down to the sawmill and make all the arrangements. You're quite old enough now to do it, but don't take your brother along. I don't trust him around machines and particularly around sawmills with those terrible saws. You be careful yourself."

I don't know why Mama had to say that. I was always careful, and the last thing in the world I would ever think of would be to take Jemmy with me when I was entrusted with something important like having a wardrobe built. I didn't complain, though; I just let it pass.

Right after I had doused the fires and left the kettles to cool, so Helga and Mama could rinse and hang up our laundry, I whisked off my apron, grabbed my old bonnet, and hurried off to the saw-mill.

I went inside just as if I did it every day. The sawmill wasn't anything more than a large open shed filled with stacked lumber, a large sharp-toothed saw, and great piles of sweet-smelling sawdust all over the place. The saw wasn't going when I went in, and I could see right away that the owner was standing at the end of the shed talking with Luke Gordon and Dutch Frank. It was serious talk, too, for all of them had dark looks on their faces, so I knew better than to butt in. I sat down on a pile of fresh-cut lumber, being careful not to get pine pitch on my dress, and waited. I could hear every word they said, for I don't think they even heard me come in.

Dutch Frank was speaking. "This here state of affairs ain't goin' to happen in Eagle," he said. "We got ways to stop it."

"But they haven't come in yet, Dutch, have they?" Luke Gordon asked. "It's only what you heard tell."

"It's true enough, though," Dutch Frank told him. "Some of us seen one or two of 'em in Spokane Falls day before yestiddy." He snorted. "They ruined the gold fields in Californy and in other places, too. They kin find gold in the cricks that no white man kin even see. And they don't spend that gold neither, like a white man would. They save it, and use it to go back to China and git buried. They don't add nothin' to any gold camp, and they ain't never any Chinamen comin' in here."

Luke Gordon, who had been silently staring at his boots, looked up at that moment and spied me. "Well, little lady," he called out. "What brings you here?"

I got up, letting on that I hadn't heard their conversation, but I knew what they were talking about all right. I'd heard Helga tell Mama, late one night when I was supposed to be asleep, how the Chinese were hated in western gold camps, but like Mama, I couldn't really see why. It didn't seem any crime to me to save money to take it back to China. After all, didn't we plan to make our fortunes and go back as soon as we could to Portland to live?

I didn't tell this to Dutch Frank, though. I just told the sawmill man what I had come for, and he nodded and treated me as if I were very grown up, asking me what kind of lumber I would like. Then he told me that he knew a carpenter in town, who would make up a wardrobe for me in jig time. While Luke Gordon and Dutch Frank looked bored, I told the sawyer how big it had to be and how deep. He nodded, and wrote everything down on a little pad. He told me not to worry, for it would be delivered finished and ready for paint by the end of the week.

Just as I started to leave, I heard Luke Gordon's

voice again, even though he didn't speak very loudly, but I do have good ears, as Mama always says. "If what you heard is true, Dutch, what I'd like to know is, who's bringin' 'em in?"

I strained my ears, but that was all I could hear, and knowing that Mama would skin me alive if she suspected I was an eavesdropper, I left the sawmill and that fascinating talk, and went back to our tent and the breakfast dishes that were waiting for me.

My wardrobe—and I must say that I really did think of it as mine—was sent over to our tent late one afternoon by the end of the week, just as the man had promised. I was so pleased with it that I began to pull things out of the carpetbags even before it was set up.

"Ann Katherine!" Mama said to me in her most chilly voice, "don't you think it would be a good idea if we waited until we painted it? You'll only have to take the things out again and put them back in the carpetbags."

I dropped a coat of Jemmy's I was just about to put away. I had forgotten all about painting my new possession.

"We'll paint it tomorrow night," said Mama, "right after we close the restaurant. Then we'll give it a few days to dry. I don't want any paint smell and stains on my dresses, and I'm sure Miss Storkersen would object too."

So that's how it went. I put things back into the carpetbags, sighed, and went over to the restaurant tent, because it was time to get things ready for dinner.

We were very busy that night. I flew back and forth with plates and cups of coffee, but I couldn't help but notice that our customers were acting very strangely. They didn't have much to say to one another, and they barely talked at all to Mama or me. They left their guns on our front table as they always did, but it was obvious, from the way they hurried over after dinner and got them strapped on again, that something was going on—and something very odd, too.

Jemmy kept hanging around the kitchen getting in Helga's way so much that Mama got exasperated and told him to go back to our tent and stay there.

"Out!" Mama ordered. "Out! And don't come back in here again tonight."

Jemmy looked sulky, but he did what Mama said. He went very slowly out of the tent, pretending that he was bored with us and that it was all his own idea to leave.

It couldn't have been more than five minutes later, though, when I had just brought some dirty plates back to the kitchen, that I heard Jemmy's voice at the tent opening. "Ann Katie!" he said in a loud whisper.

"Jemmy," I whispered back, making sure that Mama and Helga weren't watching, "you heard Mama just now. If she sees you, you'll really catch it."

"But Ann Katie," Jemmy told me, "it's awful important. It's your new wardrobe closet," he explained.

"My new wardrobe!" I said out loud, but lucky for us Helga clanged a couple of stove lids, so no one heard me. "What about my wardrobe?"

"There's somebody in it," Jemmy whispered.

When I heard this, I opened the tent flap and stared at Jemmy. He was as white as one of Mama's best napkins, while his eyes were as big as teacups.

Jemmy went on. "I heard him breathin', and it's worse'n that. He's bleedin' too. It's comin' through a crack in the wardrobe onto the dirt floor. I seen it real clear when I took the lantern over. Ann Katie, what'll we do?"

"You go get Nehemiah Spotted Horse," I said as fast as I could, "and I'll get our shotgun. I'll go get Helga too." Mama had gone through a lot of things already in Eagle City, but Helga could handle this better, I decided. "And don't you go near that tent again alone," I told him.

As Jemmy ducked his head back through the opening I heard him say, "Don't worry. I sure won't."

I rushed right over to Helga and found her putting

dirty dishes to boil in a big tub of soapy water. "Helga," I said, "can you come over to the other tent? Jemmy says that there's somebody in my new wardrobe, and he's bleeding."

Helga wheeled around and stared at me. "If you're joshin' me, little lady," she warned, "I ain't accountin' for what I'll do."

"No, I'm not, Helga," I said desperately. "Nehemiah Spotted Horse and Jemmy are waiting for us. I said we'd get the shotgun and go right away. I decided not to tell Mama."

Helga glanced at Mama who was still busy. "Well, if he's bleedin', he ain't goin' to be runnin' off," she said. "I'll tell your maw somethin' to keep her in here. She might faint or somethin' if we have to let daylight through some desperado."

We joined Nehemiah Spotted Horse and Jemmy, who were standing by the light of a palouse lantern turned down low. "Are we ready to flush out the varmint?" asked Helga. Jemmy's eyes got even bigger, but Nehemiah didn't change expression. "Well, come on," said Helga quietly, and we walked over to the second tent.

Helga put her finger to her lips, and motioned Jemmy and me back. She whispered to Nehemiah Spotted Horse, who looked at her as if he didn't understand. Then she made a motion as if to open a door, and Nehemiah finally nodded. Quickly and silently he went over to my wardrobe closet and jerked the door open.

"Come on out, you varmint, whoever you are!" cried Helga, shotgun raised and ready to fire, and looking very fierce. I was shaking like a leaf, as I held the palouser, and the light flickered all over the tent walls when I trembled.

Very slowly a man got up from the floor of my wardrobe—a small, shabbily dressed man with a thin face and slanted dark eyes. He was holding one gaunt hand to his shoulder, and we could see that he was wounded. He looked about as frightened as I've ever seen anyone look.

"Don't shoot, please, missy!" he begged Helga in a soft, strange voice. "Don't shoot!"

"Well, by Saint Olaf, if it ain't a Chinese!" Helga exclaimed, lowering the gun. "I wonder how he got up here?"

"Somebody's bringing them in," I told Helga. "I heard Dutch Frank say so a few days ago."

Helga looked at me hard as she spoke. "Dutch Frank hates Chinese." Then she said to the man, "Come out of there right now, you!"

The Chinese stepped out of my wardrobe, and stood leaning against it.

"Who are you and how did you get here?" Helga demanded.

The man bowed as much as he possibly could

without falling down. "I am Wang Erh, third son," he said. "I was brought in here by a man to work in the gold claims."

"Who was this here man?" Helga asked.

"His name was Mr. Farr," Wang Erh answered.

Jemmy gasped, but Helga silenced him with a look. "How did you get in this here tent?" she asked. "Why did you come to this place?"

"Mr. Farr said to come in here when I came to Eagle City," Wang Erh explained.

"Who shot you?" Jemmy blurted out.

"A man shot me when he saw me by his lantern," the Chinese said. "I do not understand this. Mr. Farr said that Chinese would be welcome here in Eagle City. He said that I was to come to your tent and wait for him while he took care of some business in the town. I did as he said, but I hid from the man who shot at me."

"So that's it!" said Helga. "Well, we've all been tricked real good. That varmint Farr'll be along soon enough and find you here and say that we been bringin' in Chinese right along. We're in bad trouble," she added. "It's a trap for us. They'll have this man here doin' a mid-air dance before midnight, and we'll all be run out of Eagle, while Farr'll be a hero."

"They wouldn't hang him!" cried Jemmy. "He ain't done anything wrong."

"Don't matter a bit," said Helga, biting her lip. "Some people never listen to reason. We got to get him outa here right now. We can't even patch him up. There ain't time even for Christian charity. But that's the best we can do for you, mister."

"What'll we do, Helga?" I moaned.

"I know," cried Jemmy. "I know. Nehemiah will take him out the back way, won't you Nehemiah?"

Nehemiah Spotted Horse had stood there all this time without saying a word. Now he came forward and picked up the man as easily as he could have carried Jemmy.

"Me take him away," he said.

"Where will you take him?" I asked Nehemiah, as he left our tent, Wang Erh lying limp and half-fainting against him.

"Don't know," Nehemiah Spotted Horse grunted. "But me get him away. He be safe. Maybe we go Montana—maybe Cataldo. Me go down crick and get a boat I hide there. We go now."

Jemmy and I were about to follow Nehemiah out to the creek when Helga grabbed both of us, me by the braids and Jemmy by his shirt collar. "Hold on there," she said. "You, sonny, get a shovel, and clean up that blood on the dirt, and you, girl, start hangin' up things in that wardrobe jest as fast as ever you can. Mebbe if we're lucky, they won't look inside

97

and spot anythin'. I got a feelin' it won't be long now before that Arrowsmith Farr sticks his dirty face inter our business agin."

Helga was perfectly right saying we would have visitors. Within ten minutes Mama came flying over to our tent as mad as a hornet, with her petticoats rustling as if she were walking in a high wind.

"It's that terrible Farr man, Helga!" she cried out. "He's come back, and he's brought Mr. Gordon and Mr. Dutch Frank and a lot of other men with him." Mama went right on, not noticing that anything was unusual. "That Farr had the unmitigated gall to accuse us of smuggling in a Chinese this very evening," she announced. "He told the men to search our restaurant, so they did. Now he wants to search this tent. I don't want all those people over here pawing through our private possessions. I think this is frightful!"

"Mrs.," said Helga, "this is all that Farr man's dirty doin's. He jest wants to make bad trouble for us. Let 'em look in our tent here. They ain't nothin' around here. You jest let 'em come in, and they'll soon—"

But Helga never even got to finish her words, because all at once Arrowsmith Farr pushed his way into our tent and stood there for a moment grinning at us. "Come on in, boys," he yelled. "We'll find that there Chinaman here for danged sure. They brung him in to use him to do their washin'. They think they're too high and mighty to do it theirselves."

"There's no Chinese in this tent, and there never has been," said Mama quietly to Farr. "I resent your statement, and I resent your attitude and, furthermore, I certainly don't like the idea of your searching my property."

"And *you* ain't goin' to do no searchin' either," said Helga, picking up the shotgun once more. "Dutch Frank and Luke Gordon can do it if they got a mind to."

Dutch Frank, Mr. Gordon, and several others came into the tent looking very embarrassed. They took off their hats and looked sheepishly at Mama.

Mama spoke very coldly to them. "Do look around, gentlemen," she said.

Well, there wasn't much to look at. We had no beds to hide under, and when they'd opened our trunks and peered quickly inside the wardrobe, almost as if they were afraid Mama would bite them, they were even more embarrassed.

I really shook, though, when they looked into the wardrobe, and I whispered to Helga, who still held the shotgun on Farr, "What about the stains on the bottom?"

"Don't worry," she whispered back. "I put my

shoes over 'em. I allus knew it would come in handy someday to have big feet."

Dutch Frank went up to Mama. "I'm mighty sorry, ma'am, to put you to this here trouble," he said. "There sure ain't no Chinaman here."

"Would you like to look in our carpetbags?" Jemmy burst out.

"That will do, Jemmy," stated Mama, and then she spoke to all of the men. "And now if you would please remove yourselves from my home, and take that monstrous, abominable creature with you!" And here she pointed at Farr.

"Don't you trouble yourself no more, ma'am," Luke Gordon told Mama, as he went over and laid his hand on Farr's shoulder. "This varmint has caused you enough mis'ry. He won't bother you folks again in Eagle. He sure won't."

And all the men went over and grabbed Farr, and pushed him out of the tent.

Mama was still angry. She paced up and down, her eyes flashing. "The very idea! The very idea!" she kept saying over and over. "As if we'd do such a thing!"

"Well, we got him out in time," spoke up Jemmy, before I could get my hand over his mouth.

"You did what!" cried Mama, stopping still and staring at Jemmy.

"We got the Chinese out with Nehemiah," said

Helga. "Sonny here has let the cat out of the bag, I guess. There was a Chinese hidin' here, missus. That Farr feller told him to come here. That was how Farr knew all about it. He brought the man to Eagle in the first place, and I think he done it jest to make bad times for us. It was a trap he set for all of us. He wanted us run out of this camp."

"Oh, no!" wailed Mama, plunking herself down on a trunk. "It's true then!"

"Sure, it's true," I said, "but we didn't bring him in."

"And we did save his life," Jemmy threw in.

"And we saved ourselves from bein' run out," remarked Helga. "That's somethin', missus."

Mama thought for a minute, and then passed her hand over her forehead. "Well, I'm proud of what you all did, although you took a fearful chance. I've got a good mind to pack up and go back to Portland tomorrow," she said. "I don't think my constitution will take much more of this terrifying wilderness."

"Shucks, Mama," cried Jemmy, "I like it up here. I don't want to go back to Oregon."

"In any event," Mama announced, "we shall close for a few days. My nerves are severely jangled, and we all need the rest."

"It'll do our customers some good to miss us, too," I said, "and it'll teach 'em not to listen to Arrowsmith Farr. They'll have to eat at the other places. That will be punishment enough for forcing their way in our tents. What do you think, Helga?"

"I don't know," Helga replied thoughtfully. "We mustn't kill the goose that lays the golden egg. But it would be fun to rest up a bit. Mebbe we could go up in the hills and do some berry pickin', now that Nehemiah is goin' to be gone for a while and won't be doin' it for us. I'd like to put up a big kettle of huckleberry jelly."

"We might even find O'Neil O'Neil and Timothy Clover!" I cried.

"Oh, boy!" Jemmy yelled. "Can we go, Mama?"

"You and Helga may certainly go," Mama answered, "but I know *I* won't, and I'll have to make up my mind about Ann Katherine. Young ladies from Portland do not wander about in wild country under any circumstances."

I didn't say what I was thinking, but what I thought was that Eagle City certainly wasn't Portland, and that I *would* go too.

CHAPTER 7

Timothy's Pillow

I did go, too. I wheedled and begged Mama, and promised never to be out of Helga's sight, so finally she gave up and agreed to it.

But she couldn't be budged when we tried to get her to come along. "Go yourselves," she said. "Just let me stay here and rest."

Helga winked at me when Mama talked this way, and I winked back, because both Luke Gordon and Montana Bellows had rushed over the next morning to apologize to Mama. Mama wasn't very friendly toward them, and stuck to her guns that they had trespassed on her property, but she did warm up a little when she learned that Arrowsmith Farr had been run out of Eagle City and warned never to come back.

I was pleased to hear them say that. It made me feel better to learn that they were sure we had seen the last of our enemy, but I still couldn't help but wonder whether he would come back into our lives again.

Jemmy was very excited to be going out huckleberry picking. But the main reason he wanted to go was that he hoped that he would find Timothy Clover. The minute Helga and I were ready to leave, loaded down with bedrolls, supplies, and pots and pans, Jemmy piped up, "What direction do you think O'Neil O'Neil took, Helga?"

Helga pursed her lips and thought for a minute before she answered. "Sonny, I think O'Neil said he was goin' east toward Montana Territory, but that ornery little dickens has been gone long enough to be in Alaska Territory by now."

"Are there huckleberries in the east?" Jemmy asked anxiously.

"Sure, sonny, the hills is blue with 'em," Helga said kindly. "You want to go east, I s'pose?"

"Yes, I do," Jemmy replied. "That's where Timothy Clover is, I bet."

"Well, we'll head east then," Helga stated, hitching up a pack strap on her shoulder. "You two run and kiss your maw good-by, and then we'll light out toward Thompson Falls."

We did as Helga ordered, and rushed in to kiss Mama, who was lying down with a cloth, soaked in vinegar and water, over her eyes. She lifted it and opened one eye and peered at me.

"Ann Katherine," she said, "look out for your little brother."

"I will, Mama," I promised her. "We'll be back by noon tomorrow. What could happen to Jemmy?"

"What couldn't happen to him is more to the point," Mama replied, putting the cloth down over her eyes again. "Take care of yourself too, and Jemmy, you obey Miss Storkersen, do you hear?"

We tiptoed out of the tent and ran, a coffee pot, a skillet, and two empty lard-bucket berry pails rattling in the bedroll on my back, to catch up with Helga, who was halfway down the street.

We waved to Luke Gordon, standing in front of his freight office, and then we were out on the trail that ran eastward from Eagle City.

"I wish we had Nehemiah Spotted Horse along with us," said Jemmy. "I'll bet he could trail Timothy Clover for me."

"Wonder where Nehemiah is right now," Helga mused, not answering Jemmy. "I guess he must have got the Chinese man out all right. If he didn't, we would sure have heard about it by now."

"People up here are certainly funny, Helga," I said. "I don't see why they hate Chinese so much."

"Well," Helga grunted, pushing a branch out of

her way as we left the main trail for a much narrower one, "they ain't so much diff'runt from anybody else, I guess, jest a little stronger in their idees and doin's. People get queer notions. I give up tryin' to understand 'em. You people who hail from cities never let on what you're thinkin'. You jest smile and nod your head, and nobody knows what's goin' on inside you. The people who live in Eagle call a spade a spade, when they don't call it a dirty shovel. Mebbe you city folks don't like Chinese people either, but you don't hang 'em or run 'em out. You jest work 'em for no money, and you make 'em live all cooped up together in tight places. Who's to say who does the worst by 'em?"

Helga stopped, and looked all around her. We were now quite a distance from the main trail, and there wasn't a thing in sight but hillsides. "This is where I get rid of this doggoned bustle," she said, and began to fumble at her waist.

I watched, horrified, as Helga began taking off her skirt. Was she going huckleberry picking in her petticoats? "Helga!" I cried, shocked, and when she had taken off her skirt and unhooked and untied her bustle, I was even more shocked. I cried out once more, "Helga!"

There she stood, wearing a pair of man's black corduroy trousers. Jemmy clapped his hand over his mouth, so he wouldn't laugh. Helga was a shocking sight, but she was even funnier than she was shocking.

"Go on and laugh, sonny," she told Jemmy. "Bet you never saw a lady dressed like this before. Anybody who'd go hikin' in a bustle and a long skirt is a plain idjit, that's all!"

She plunked the bustle inside the skirt, and rolled it up, tying the skirt onto her bedroll. "That's so if we meet anybody on the trail, I can duck into the bushes and get duded up agin," she explained. "I wouldn't want to make any prospector's mule blush if he saw me in pants."

Without another word Helga swung back on the eastward trail again, and we began to walk. We walked uphill and downhill for hours, and examined hundreds of huckleberry bushes. But none seemed really ripe yet, although many of them had little red berries on them that would make for good picking later.

But we still didn't find any berries big enough to pick, so we stopped for the night at the foot of a steep hill.

"Do you think we'll find huckleberries tomorrow, Helga?" Jemmy asked her. "Do you think there'll be any berries around a crick somewheres, so I can do some panning?"

"Did you bring that wash basin of Spotted Horse's?" Helga asked.

"I sure did," Jemmy said. "O'Neil showed me how to pan for gold back in Eagle."

"Well, sonny," Helga said severely, "don't get your hopes up too high. I've had the feelin' for a couple of days now that these here hills is jest about panned out."

"What makes you say that?" I put in.

"People are beginnin' to leave Eagle," she said. "You don't notice it much yet, but there'll soon be a rush gittin' out, jest the way it was a rush gittin' in."

"But how can we live if no one eats at our place?" asked Jemmy.

"You can't," she replied, starting to build a fire and motioning to me to take off my pack. "But your maw has made enough money already, even if she won't admit it. She's done real well by herself—a lot better'n she would have done teachin'. I dunno how she could ever have got an idee in her head to come up here and teach school. But that's none of my bus'ness. Anyhow, Scott and Storkersen is goin' to bust up pretty soon, so you folks'll go back to Oregon."

"Helga, what will you do?" I wailed, worried by her words.

"I'll go to Thompson Falls or to some other gold camp in the territories," she said. "That's if I don't run inter O'Neil agin."

I thought I was going to cry, but I held back the tears and only sniffled. I knew how she felt about tears. "Oh, Helga, we'll miss you so much. There's nobody like you in the whole world."

"Well, don't carry on so," she said. "The camp ain't folded yet, and I could be wrong about it."

"Does Mama know?" asked Jemmy.

"Nope, I haven't told her what I think about things yet. Thought I'd tell her when we go back to Eagle. She needs the rest right now, without me loadin' her down with bad news. She's been through a lot already."

We ate a very sad dinner that night, although Helga was nearly as good a cook over a campfire as with a wood stove. Then we took out our bedrolls and got into them and lay on our backs looking up at the stars, which were very bright and close to us. But as I drifted off to sleep, I thought I heard someone calling from far away.

"Helga," I said sleepily, "do you hear something?"

"I sure do," was her comment, "And I got the deer gun real handy here, too, in case it's one of them two-legged varmints."

"It isn't Farr?" I asked in fear.

"Nope, that man wouldn't call out," Helga replied. "He'd sneak up."

"Who can it be?" I asked.

"It's prob'ly some prospector who's seen our fire

and got lonesome, I bet," she answered. "It gets danged lonesome up here alone. People need other people. You got to jaw with somebody else now and then, or you get funny in the head. These prospectors'll talk the ear off you when they first get back from the hills. They jest can't help it."

Helga stood up and called out, "Hello," as loudly as she could, and seconds later we heard an answer. Helga called again, and was answered once more, and this time it sounded closer. Soon we heard the noise of someone slipping and sliding over the carpet of dried pine needles not far from us.

"Do you have any coffee?" came a voice out of the night, and a small black figure came stumbling up to our fire.

Jemmy leaped out of his blankets and clutched at me, while I saw Helga start and put the deer gun on the ground.

"Holy saints, it is herself and the little ones," cried O'Neil O'Neil, as he staggered onto the pile of Helga's blankets and fell down. "Put the coffee on for the prodigal son, me darlin's."

O'Neil O'Neil was a sight. He carried a bedroll on his back and, judging from the look on his face, it was all he could do to carry it. He was much thinner. His clothes were torn and dirty, and he looked completely worn out. His beard and red mustache had grown long, and they were a ragged-looking sight too.

"Where've you been, O'Neil?" Helga demanded almost angrily, throwing some sticks on the fire.

"Don't interrogate me now, dear one," he croaked. "Put something into this bottomless pit I once referred to as my stomach. I've not seen food except berries for two days, and I dream of coffee. I smelled your coffee for ten miles, and it led me to you."

Jemmy couldn't wait any longer. He rushed over to O'Neil and asked, "Where's my mule? What have you done with Timothy Clover?"

"He's gone," O'Neil said, shaking his head. "I'm sorry, boy, but two mornings ago the poor beast fell into a ravine with what was left of my supplies. There was a roaring torrent at the bottom, and when I got down the sides of the ravine to look for him, he was gone. He must have been swept away. Oh, it's been a sorry expedition this time—no gold, not one nugget, and the finest, sweetest pack beast in Idaho Territory gone to his reward."

Jemmy stood for a long while and finally began to cry. "Do you think there's a mule heaven?" he asked Helga.

"I'm sure there is," Helga soothed him. "He's up there right now, wearin' golden horseshoes."

Jemmy cried all the harder when she said this, and

I felt a big painful lump in my throat, too. "Don't cry, Jemmy," I said. "Mama will get you another mule when she hears what happened to Timothy Clover."

"There's only one mule in the world for me," he wailed. "I don't want any other mule, and don't you ever mention his name again." Then Jemmy flung himself down on his bedroll and cried, while Helga sliced bacon to fry for O'Neil.

"What can we do?" I asked O'Neil, going over and sitting down on a log beside him.

"Alas, we can only let him weep," O'Neil replied bitterly. "He's just a lad now, and he won't be allowed to cry much longer. That's the way this sad world goes."

"Are the streams jest about panned out?" Helga asked quietly.

"That they are, me love," he replied. "Once more the golden luck of the O'Neil has eluded him. I have lost the child's beloved beast, and I have betrayed the trust of all of you."

"Oh, it ain't the end of the world," chided Helga. "There are always new gold fields openin' up. You shouldn't blame yourself for somethin' you couldn't help. Here, eat some bread and bacon, and drink some coffee. There never was a thing in the world that was so dreary a cup of coffee at the right time couldn't sweeten it up."

"I don't suppose you've got a lightnin' flash any-where?" O'Neil asked Helga. "I thought you might have one in case of snake bite. There are timber rattlers in these hills, you know."

"Nope, I don't carry such stuff," Helga replied. "You know I don't touch it, and ain't never goin' to neither."

"The trouble with you, my darlin'," went on O'Neil, looking sadly into the fire, "is that you are a coffee-drinking Swede, and I am an Irishman with other tastes."

"We can get along anyhow," Helga said, laughing, and looking fondly at O'Neil.

We went to bed again as soon as O'Neil O'Neil had finished his bacon and bread, but were awakened soon after the sun rose by Helga's clattering of pots and pans. "Rise and shine," she called out to us. "Go down to the crick to wash, and git right back here. We got to pick huckleberries this mornin', and git back to Eagle before Mrs. Scott sends out a posse after us."

Jemmy got up, looking red-eyed and unhappy, and refused to eat any breakfast. He did not speak, and I didn't mention Timothy Clover to him.

"O'Neil," asked Helga, "did you see any good patches of huckleberries in your wanderin'? You said last night you lived off berries for two days."

"That I did," he said, "and I know where there

are berries. The hillsides are as blue as your eyes with them in a gulch just over the next ridge."

We set out the moment we had eaten, O'Neil in the lead, followed by Helga and me, with Jemmy bringing up the rear. We didn't walk for too long, and it wasn't such hard going either. O'Neil knew the way quite well, and said that he'd been this way many times on his prospecting trips.

Finally we entered the gulch and looked around us. It wasn't much different from any other gulch we'd been seeing all along, but there were huckleberry bushes on the slopes of the hills, and they were purple-blue with large ripe berries, just as O'Neil had said they would be.

I took off my pack, got out the buckets, and gave one to Helga. "Jemmy," I said, "get your bucket out of your pack."

"I don't want to do any berry picking," he stated.

"How about doing a little panning with me?" O'Neil asked him. "It might take your mind off things."

"Oh, all right," Jemmy answered, without any real interest in his voice. "I guess I might as well do something." He put his pack down, and took out Nehemiah Spotted Horse's washbowl.

"Now that's the ticket," exclaimed O'Neil. "We'll hunt us up a stream, and see if we can get any color today."

"Color?" I asked. "What's that?"

"Gold," replied O'Neil. "That's what we call gold flakes."

"Oh, come on," Helga broke in. "Let's get to the huckleberries, little lady. We ain't got all day to stand here and jaw."

I followed her obediently along the gulch up a slope toward the bushes, while O'Neil and Jemmy headed toward the left to look for a creek.

"Do you suppose Jemmy will ever get over his mule?" I asked Helga, as I began to pick, staining my fingers blue. The berries made rattling noises in the bottom of the bucket.

"It's hard to say," she replied. "He may get over him, but he sure won't ever forget that critter."

"Are you glad to see O'Neil again?" I asked slyly, in my most innocent voice, for I had noticed that as soon as she got up she had worn her skirt and bustle. I wondered how she had ever managed to get them on in a roll of blankets.

"I might be," she replied, "and then agin I might not be. Pick berries, and don't be so nosey about my business."

I had to smile at this, and I didn't want Helga to see me grinning, so I moved away from her to the other side of the large bush.

And there I got the shock of my life!

There lay Timothy Clover. He was on his side,

stretched out in the sun, his head pillowed on a large flat rock, with the packsaddle and bags missing.

"Helga!" I cried out. "It's Jemmy's mule!"

Helga came hustling around the bush, her pail swinging in her hand. "It ain't possible," she cried. "The poor beast is dead."

"No, he's not dead," I corrected her. "See how his sides move, and I saw him twitch his tail a minute ago. He's sound asleep."

"It takes a lot to kill off a mule," Helga breathed. "Wait until sonny hears about this. You go get him."

Without another word I dropped the bucket and began to run. I could see Jemmy and O'Neil as little figures way off in the distance on another hillside, and I called and called to them, still running, until Jemmy finally turned around and waved. I waved back and motioned for him and O'Neil to return. At last they seemed to understand, but they came so slowly that I thought they'd never get there. I was about to explode.

As soon as they were within earshot, I called out, "Jemmy, we found Timothy Clover. He's all right. He's asleep up on that hill."

"How is he? Is he all right? Is he sick?" Jemmy asked, all excited.

"I didn't ask him," I said. "He was asleep, so I didn't wake him up."

"I'll go get him up!" cried Jemmy, and leaped away from us toward the hillside. "I'll wake him up!"

O'Neil laughed as he and I walked across the gulch. "Well, I'm certainly happy that my misadventure had a joyous outcome," he remarked.

"If you could only find a lot of gold, everything would be fine, Mr. O'Neil."

"Ah, yes," O'Neil sighed, "but that's too forlorn a hope. Gold is not for me."

We climbed the slope, and there stood Jemmy and the miraculously saved animal. Jemmy had his head buried in Timothy Clover's bristly mane, and was whispering to him. Even Timothy Clover looked happy—or at least I thought he did. Mules don't have much expression.

"Ain't love grand?" Helga commented, pointing to them. "But it sure don't pick any huckleberries."

I started over with Helga to another bush, while O'Neil sat on the ground and took out his pipe. He tapped it on the rock that Timothy Clover had used for a pillow, and then he tapped it again. The rock was a reddish color and seemed to crumble as O'Neil rapped on it.

"That's funny," I heard him say. He frowned and put his pipe away, taking out a knife he carried in a sheath at his belt. Then he sat down on his knees and brushed at the stone with his hands. He began to dig at the rock with the knife.

"By all the holy saints in heaven!" he cried out. "I do believe the O'Neil has done it at last."

"Done what?" Helga asked, coming over to him.

"Look here!" he said, pointing to the rock, his hand shaking. "Do you see what I see?"

"All I see is a shiny gray streak in a rock," said I. "What are we supposed to see?"

"Do you know what this is, little lady?" he asked. "Do you have any idea in the world what you are gazing at?"

"No," I confessed. "I don't know. It isn't gold, is it?"

O'Neil shook his head. "No, that's not gold—I told you there was no gold in O'Neil's life. But I forgot in my blindness that there might be something else."

"For heaven's sake, man, what could that be?" barked Helga.

"Galena," said O'Neil softly, "that's what."

"And what is that?" she asked.

"It's lead and something else."

"What else?" I cried, staring once more at the streak of metal.

"Silver!" said O'Neil, getting to his feet and tilting his hat at a jauntier angle. "Dear ladies, you are looking at the richest hunk of silver-lead ore I've ever seen."

"Well, what is it worth?" asked Helga, when she recovered from her surprise.

"If we're at all in luck," went on O'Neil, "it'll be worth millions. We're rich. We're rich beyond our wildest dreams! Perhaps we've got a whole mountain of galena under our feet right here. The gold may be gone, but I'm going to wager that this gulch and these canyons are going to see a silver strike to rival the Comstock Lode."

"Silver!" I said softly to myself. "I never even thought of silver."

"Almost as good as gold," Helga said happily. "It jest takes more of it."

"Me darlin'," O'Neil addressed Helga, "I shall festoon you with diamonds and pearls, and take you to San Francisco with me as my bride."

"Shucks," said Helga, "jest buy me a new fryin' pan and put me in my own kitchen, little man, and you won't want to go to San Francisco."

I was too excited to realize that I had been witness to a real proposal of marriage. "We've got a silver mine!" I said. "What'll we call it?"

O'Neil stood for a moment, thinking. "If we are to follow time-honored tradition," he said, "when the word gets out, we must say that the mule, Timo-

119

thy Clover, discovered the lode. We must say that he strayed away and wandered up against a hill of pure silver, dazzling our eyes in the sunlight. Or we could say that he kicked up a rock with his hoof and exposed a magnificent hill of ore. We must never say he was sleeping on the job. That would never do. A man must live and abide by the legends. We should call it the Timothy Clover Mine."

"I don't like that," I said. "It doesn't sound right."

Just then Jemmy came down toward us, leading his mule. I don't think he even realized we had just become rich. All he knew was that Timothy Clover was back. "Look at him, Ann Katie!" Jemmy crowed. "He falls into a ravine, and there ain't a mark on him. This here is sure some mule all right. Good old Timothy, good old lucky Clover!"

Helga nudged O'Neil. "There's your name, O'Neil," she announced. "Sonny jest named our mine. It'll be the Lucky Clover."

CHAPTER 8

Silver Fever

We hurried back to Eagle City just as fast as we could—forgetting about the huckleberry picking. I was happy that I had the silver strike to keep me occupied, because I would have felt quite lonesome if I hadn't. Jemmy walked along whispering fond nothings to Timothy Clover, and O'Neil O'Neil and Helga had words only for each other.

I did get to ask O'Neil, though, when we sat down to rest once, how he knew that there was galena in Timothy Clover's pillow, and he told me that when that kind of ore was exposed to the air it oxidized and turned a reddish color. That was why the tales of great sheets of gleaming silver were all wrong.

"What do we have to do now that we've found silver?" I asked him.

"Well," replied O'Neil, taking his pipe out of his mouth and knocking the ashes against the trunk of a tree, "first thing of all, little lady, is to keep perfectly quiet about this discovery of ours. The word will get out soon enough, believe me, and that gulch will be swarming with prospectors. I'm going to go back there just as soon as I get supplies, and I'll stake a claim then. Helga can come back with me and get the information, and she'll file on the Lucky Clover for all of us."

"How exactly do you stake a claim?" I asked him.

"We'll have to mark out the boundaries of the Lucky Clover mine, and put up stakes with written markers on them. Then we'll file that description with the United States government, and the claim is ours, if we keep it up according to law. Then I'll have to squat up there," he went on. "Someone will have to stay at the mine to guard it, if she's half as rich as I think she is."

"What could anyone do to a mine?"

"The only real thing they can do until we get enough money to sink a shaft, is jump our claim, move our markers or destroy them, and take it over. Then they'd keep us off the property with guns."

"But that's dishonest!" I exclaimed.

"It's not only dishonest. It's about the most dangerous thing you can try to do hereabouts, except steal a horse." O'Neil rambled on, "I put those ore samples in my pack to send off to the assayer in Spokane Falls. There's not much doubt in my mind, but if we're going to interest capital in the Lucky

Clover, we've got to have some bait to dangle in front of them, and there's nothing like an interesting assayer's report for that purpose."

"Do we have to have a lot of money to get started?" I asked.

"Silver mining is not entirely like gold mining," he replied. "You don't pan silver; you sink shafts and tunnels. It's expensive to get silver cut. It isn't any one-man operation by a long ways, little lady."

"I guess we won't be working the mine ourselves then," I said. "I guess we'd better consider selling the Lucky Clover before we get in too deep."

"That's real good thinkin'," Helga threw in. "From what O'Neil here says, we won't be able to do much ourselves but start a hole in the ground."

O'Neil nodded. "We'll hang on to it until we get the right price, though," he said.

We made it back to Eagle City in good order, and Helga propelled O'Neil directly to our tents, although he cast several longing glances at the saloons as we passed by. I was pretty sure that O'Neil O'Neil had seen the last of gum ticklers for a long time, if Helga had anything to say about his future.

Mama was up and around and looking much more rested than before, and she even seemed happy to see Timothy Clover again, although I can't say that she felt the same way about O'Neil O'Neil's turning up once more. We all went inside our tent. O'Neil swore everyone to deepest secrecy the moment he entered, and mysteriously tied down the tent flaps and lit the kerosene lantern, although it was still daylight. Mama was quite mystified and a little bit annoyed, but she went along with it.

"Dear madam," O'Neil addressed Mama, "we are about to divulge something of the greatest importance to you."

"And what could that be?" Mama asked.

"Miss Storkersen, myself, and your two remarkable children—and thereby yourself—are about to become wealthy."

"Now what do you mean by such foolish hocus-pocus?" Mama asked crossly.

"I mean, dear lady," he went on, opening his pack and taking out a chunk of galena ore, "that I have found silver, and I do believe that I have found it in great quantities."

"I congratulate you and wish you well, Mr. O'Neil," Mama said, "but I certainly don't see how my family is implicated or what Miss Storkersen has to do with this."

"They were my benefactors—my grubstakers, in other words. They share in my good fortune," O'Neil announced in a ringing voice.

"Jemmy and Ann Katherine!" Mama exclaimed.

"Your daughter and Miss Storkersen gave me cash for supplies, while, as you know, your son donated the services of his mule, an animal without equal. I have reckoned up the accounts. Miss Storkersen is the owner of a quarter of the Lucky Clover, and your children share a quarter also. Half the mine belongs to me, inasmuch as I am the discoverer and will be the developer."

Mama sat down. For a moment I thought she was going to have something severe to say to Jemmy and me, but she only looked at O'Neil in disbelief. "And exactly what does all this mean?" she asked him.

"It signifies that we are all wealthy," said O'Neil, "wealthy beyond our wildest dreams. To use a term employed by the unlettered, we have struck it rich. You came up here to teach school, but teachers do not make fortunes, even though what they impart is pure gold. Your restaurant has given you an adequate reward for much hard labor, but now you can recline in the velvet lap of luxury."

Mama shook her head, then turned to speak to Helga. "Helga," she asked, "are you all a little mad today? Has Mr. O'Neil been in Dutch Frank's place?"

"Nope," Helga replied, chuckling, "he sure ain't. I saw to that, missus. He's tellin' you true. Ain't he the one, though?"

"Well, he certainly is the one, not that I know what that means," Mama commented with a sigh. "It's a little overwhelming to be suddenly told that one is wealthy beyond one's wildest dreams."

"We'll get used to it, Mama," Jemmy piped up. "It won't take long. Just you wait and see."

Helga and O'Neil left early the next morning, and Helga was back before that evening with all the information they needed to file the claim. Timothy Clover did not go with O'Neil this time. Jemmy refused to let him out of his sight, and O'Neil did not ask for the mule. As a matter of fact, Helga rounded up another one for O'Neil in a very short time. Timothy Clover did not like the other mule at all. He laid back his ears and grinned wickedly at him, but the new mule wasn't around long enough for a battle to begin.

Helga hurried right off to file our claim, and came back chuckling. "You should have seen their eyes bulgin' when I filed our claim on the Lucky Clover," she told Mama and me. "The stampede's goin' to start any time now. There ain't no keepin' a secret once the filin's been done. There's goin' to be a rush for that gulch where O'Neil found galena. He won't be lonesome up there for long."

"I don't see anyone doing much rushing about," said Mama, looking out the flap of the restaurant tent.

"I jest got back from filin'," Helga explained. "You got to give 'em time to get supplies on their mules. The rush will be at the stores right now. It's

126

real funny to see how a stampede commences. The word gets out, and goes from mouth to mouth at first. Then everybody gits ready to go, but they don't talk much about that. No one wants anyone else to know where he's off to. By early mornin' you'll see 'em goin' out to the hills by the dozens, pretendin' that they're jest goin' out to try a new stream for color. By tomorrow night doggoned near every inch of that gulch'll be staked out and claimed. You'll see!"

"Will this affect our business?" Mama asked, and I knew that she was worried.

"You're darn tootin'," Helga replied. "We'll lose most of our customers, except for the town people, and we'll lose them soon enough."

"Well, what can we do then?" cried Mama.

Helga laughed and picked me up, swinging me off my feet as if I were a baby. "We pick up and move, missus," she announced. "We'll go, tents and all, to where the silver is, and we'll set up another eatin' house there. If we pack up and leave inside of the week, we'll jest be able to make it in time before the saloons and the dance halls git there."

Mama sat down at one of our tables and sighed. It seemed to me that Mama had done nothing else since we came up to Idaho Territory. "It's a good thing we didn't open up again, I suspect. Moving a hot stove wouldn't be easy. But will Mr. Webster let us keep these rented tents when we go, do you suppose?"

"He'll be movin' too," cried Helga. "You can't be a rental agent with nobody to rent to, and Eagle'll be a ghost town in ten days. It sure seems I'm goin' to marry up with O'Neil in some place other'n Eagle."

Mama stared at Helga. "You're going to marry O'Neil O'Neil?" she almost shouted. "You're really going to marry that man!"

Helga wasn't bothered or insulted. "Sure I am. I ain't gettin' no younger, and he suits me fine. We jest decided it. He was only waitin' until he struck it rich to ask me."

"Will you leave us when you get married?" I piped up.

"Naw, not for a long time," answered Helga, "not until we can set up housekeepin' right and proper. By the time we get hitched I don't want to be livin' in any more drafty old tents. And besides, until we sell it, O'Neil will have to live at the Lucky Clover. We're goin' to do this up in real fine style, you bet."

"Helga Storkersen," Mama said severely, "are you aware of the fact that there is no minister of the gospel in this area?"

"Oh, sure, I know that. We'll have to wait until we get ourselves a preacher. And in order to get us a preacher, we got to get a church, and to get a church, we got to get a pot of money together. But I've got it all figgered out."

By this time Mama and I were open-mouthed. "We can't build a church and get a minister all alone," said I.

"Of course not," was Helga's almost scornful answer. "But I know where there'll be lots of money pretty soon."

"And where is that, pray?" Mama asked.

"In a little while there'll be a railroad in here to carry out the silver ore to the smelters and mills. Then there'll be payrolls and money in the miners' pockets, and it'll be real easy to get money for a church and preacher for the families that'll be comin' in with the railroad."

"But how?"

"You and I, missus, we'll jest go from saloon to saloon with a hat and ask for donations. There won't be nothin' to it. They'll give money to us all right," Helga said calmly.

Mama turned pea green. I thought she was going to faint. She pressed her hands to her forehead and moaned.

"Don't take on so, missus," said Helga. "It's all for a real good cause. It ain't as if you went into a saloon for a gum tickler. You'll be doin' somethin' real fine, you know. I figger you ought to get us a good bit of gold from Dutch Frank and Montana Bellows, seein' as how they both admire you and eat here all the time."

"I just couldn't do such a thing. What would my friends back in Portland think if they knew I'd ever set foot in a saloon? They'd just die if they knew," Mama said in a flat, little voice.

"Sure, you can. You can do it when you know that it's for a church in the new town. And if they don't give real high, wide, and handsome, I'll burn their beans for 'em. You jest see if I don't."

We moved by the end of the week, as Helga had prophesied, and along with us went every other business in Eagle City. The eastward trails were choked with mule trains, laden down with folded tents, sawmill equipment, gambling tables, saloon chairs, and everything else Eagle City had, except the few wooden buildings themselves.

"Where do you suppose that dratted Nehemiah is?" Helga asked me the morning we left. "Do you suppose he went back to the reservation once he got the Chinese man out? We could sure use some help here."

"I wouldn't be at all surprised to find Nehemiah Spotted Horse waiting for us at the Lucky Clover," I said. "He's O'Neil's friend, and he just came here to help us when O'Neil wanted to go off prospecting, remember? He could have heard about the silver strike and gone up to the new town."

"All I can say then," commented Helga, jamming her blue-velvet dress into a carpetbag, "is that he has a funny way of doin' things. Tryin' to understand that man is worse'n tryin' to understand anybody else."

"Did you ever think, Helga, that you might always have Nehemiah around, since he's O'Neil's friend?"

Helga rubbed at her nose. "Mebbe I can marry Nehemiah off too, along with your maw. That would settle everythin'. Trouble is I don't know anyone who's right for him."

I laughed and closed a carpetbag. "Come on, Helga," I said. "This is the last thing to go. We'd better get out of here before the men let the tent fall down right on top of us."

She eyed me keenly. "Don't think I'm joshin' you, little lady. Your maw *will* get hitched up here, I bet."

"Well, what person do you fancy?" I asked.

"Myself, I like Montana Bellows. But I think the missus likes Luke Gordon better. He's more of a real dude, I guess, and though he don't think as fancy and eddicated as your maw and O'Neil, his language ain't as bad as Montana's. That would count with your maw. Who knows, though? We're goin' to have all the men in the silver camp samplin' our home cookin'. Mebbe it'll be somebody brand new, who'll come along and sweep her right off her feet. I'm gettin' mighty tired of seein' the missus runnin' around lookin' like an old black crow in those widder's weeds of hers."

I didn't reply to Helga. I wasn't too eager to see Mama remarry. In some ways it seemed disloyal to the memory of Papa. But I *was* tired of wearing mourning and of seeing her in it, so I had to agree with Helga.

Finally we went out into the street, and stood while our things were loaded onto the mules. We watched Eagle City die. Everyone was on the move. While we stood there, we saw Dutch Frank's entire saloon go by on the backs of several dozen mules. Then Mr. Webster rode by on his horse, and tipped his hat to us, and a few moments later Luke Gordon came up and asked if he could help us move.

"There's nothin' we need 'cept customers when we get there," Helga called loudly. "Jest pass the word around that Scott and Storkersen are goin' to put out the best grub you ever stored away in jest a few days from now. It'll have to be sowbelly and beans until the stores get runnin' and supplyin' us, but we'll get goin' full blast jest as soon as we can."

As Luke Gordon rode away, Jemmy appeared, accompanied by Timothy Clover. The mule carried two large gunny sacks on his back. "I got all our root vegetables," Jemmy told us. "There's no use leavin' 'em here for the jack rabbits."

"That's good, sonny," Helga complimented him. "We shouldn't leave good food behind. We're goin' to need it pretty bad for a while."

Jemmy looked dismayed. "Oh, I didn't do it for us," he said. "My mule here has had a real bad time, and he likes carrots."

"Heaven give me strength!" I cried out. "We can all get scurvy, but Timothy Clover has to have his carrots."

Jemmy defended himself. "This mule is making us rich, and you don't even want to give him a carrot now and then. Who found the Lucky Clover mine anyhow? Did you?"

I knew that I was beaten already in this argument, so I was more than happy to see Mama come along with her bonnet and gloves on. I knew she would end Jemmy's silly comments. He was getting worse all the time.

"Oh, how I detest moving!" Mama complained. "I'm glad we're going to walk, though. I don't want to see a horse again for a long time. Just coming up here from Cataldo Flats was enough for me. And seeing to it that those cackling chickens got crated and onto the backs of our mules was almost more than I could bear. I hope we can make our fortunes immediately in the new camp, and go back to civilization at once. I've noticed that all of Eagle City's desperadoes are heading for the silver fields, and I've spied some new, very rough-looking men."

"Oh, it won't be much different up there," Helga said. "We're goin' to be mighty busy runnin' our eatin' house and helpin' O'Neil develop the mine on our days off."

"I have absolutely no intention of working any mine," Mama stated flatly. "I came here to teach school, not pan for silver."

"You don't pan for silver," corrected Jemmy. "You use a pick and shovel, and you dig it out."

Mama shuddered while she retied her bonnet strings. "Well, I particularly don't intend to do any of that," she said. "If you want to fool around in the mine, you may, but I don't intend to set foot in it."

"And you won't neither," Helga said. "No woman sets foot in a mine, you know. The men think it's real bad luck. Sonny here'll be the only one of us who'll git inside the Lucky Clover. We'll have to help on the outside."

Jemmy was as happy as I was disappointed. "I'll get O'Neil to show me how to use giant powder and dynamite, and I'll blast out that old galena ore like nothin' you ever saw."

"You will not do any such thing," Mama warned.

"If you so much as go near explosives, you will go right back to Portland to boarding school, and you'll go without that mule, too."

This made Jemmy look sour, but he didn't say another word.

Mama turned to Helga. "Helga, do you think this new camp will be as lawless and wild as Eagle City? Will we be in danger there?"

"No more'n here," Helga responded. "When the railroad comes, it'll be better. Steadier people will come in then. There may be one thing we got to watch out for, though."

"What's that?" Mama asked, a shadow crossing her face.

"Well, they told Arrowsmith Farr not to come back to the gold camps, but they didn't say nothin' about silver camps."

"That's true," I said softly.

"It ain't so likely he'll show up," Helga went on, frowning. "But he follows the strikes, people tell me, and it'll be mighty temptin' to that timber rattler to see if he can't strike it rich, too. We'd better be ready jest in case, and keep the shotgun right handy to us."

Mama bit her lip and looked to where the men were collapsing our tents. "I won't think about that now," she said. "I just remembered something else. We forgot the lilac bush and Mr. Bellows' rose.

Jemmy, if you could find a spade on one of the mules, would you please dig up our bushes. Perhaps Timothy Clover would consider carrying them for us. I don't want to leave them here." She looked at Helga and smiled a sad little smile. "Oh, Helga," she asked, "how many times do you think we'll have to move these poor little bushes before we have our fortunes made? How many moves can they stand?"

Helga put her arm around Mama's shoulder and squeezed her. "If they get enough tender care and lots of lovin', they can take lots of moves," she said. "They're a lot like folks that way. I'll tell you what, missus, you always keep a lilac bush by the front flap of our tent, and I'll always keep the shotgun handy. We'll get by."

CHAPTER 9

Winter in Wallace

"What is the new town called?" I asked Mama, as we entered the gulch.

Mama shaded her eyes with her hand and looked out over the little valley, dotted everywhere with tents and with blue plumes of wood smoke, strong in the cool air. Summer had passed, and I remembered I had heard that the first snow always fell by Halloween. I sighed. Much as I liked Idaho Territory, I didn't care much for what O'Neil O'Neil had said about the long, bitterly cold winters.

Mama answered my question. "I don't think it has a name yet, Ann Katherine."

"But how do places get named?" asked Jemmy.

Helga got behind Timothy Clover and gave him a strong push, and then as the mule began to move along again, she came up to us. "They name towns after somebody or other who lives in 'em, or after presidents or somebody else."

"So many places in the West have the word *city* in their names," I said.

"It's jest wishful thinkin'," said Helga. "They want to be a city, I guess, but most of 'em never do make it. The people jest keep movin' on."

We found a good site for the new restaurant, and Helga put up the tents at once, with Jemmy helping with the stakes and lines. We couldn't hire anyone to help us do this, and we felt we were lucky to have the men in our pack train stay long enough to unload the cookstoves. They were wild to try their luck at prospecting, so the minute they had dumped our things on the ground they rushed off with their mules.

Helga looked after them, scowling. "Good riddance!" she grunted. "They've got silver fever all right. They wouldn't have been of any use to us anyway."

We all went to work, and it wasn't long before we were pretty well settled, except for taking things from our carpetbags and hanging them in our wardrobe. Finally Helga dumped a huge bag of dried beans into one of our washtubs to soak overnight.

"We're back to the danged old beans," Jemmy said in disgust.

"It won't be for long," Mama told him. "The stores will be here soon, and then we can serve the same menu as at Eagle City."

138

"It sure don't take long for people to get settled," said Helga. "Did you see the saloons and dance halls goin' full blast already?"

"How could I possibly miss it?" said Mama. "It was deafening and disgusting. I don't see how such nice men as Montana Bellows and Mr. Dutch Frank can tolerate such a life."

"Luke Gordon isn't a saloon owner," I put in. "He owns two mule trains and a part interest in the sawmill, and he's interested in getting a railroad in here."

"Well, we can guess who'll be showin' your maw the new camp by moonlight," Helga said, chuckling.

"Fiddlesticks!" cried Mama, and she shook a table-cloth with a loud snap, her whole face pink with a blush.

Luke Gordon called on us that first night we were in the new town, to ask us all to a town meeting. "They're going to name the place," he announced. "We have to find a name that suits the post office. Maybe, when we get a railroad in here, we'll get better mail service."

"That's quite true," Mama agreed. "It's a frightful state of affairs. It takes a month to get a letter from Portland."

I looked at Mama in surprise. She hadn't written a single letter since we came to Eagle City in the spring, but when Mr. Gordon looked so pleased at her agreement, I understood. It did seem that he had the inside track, for she tried to please him.

We bundled ourselves in heavy clothes, shawls, and capes and went out, leaving Helga seated near our supplies with the shotgun under her arm. We walked toward the new saloon, while men, carrying lanterns and pine-knot torches, came from all directions in the tent city.

Dutch Frank mounted a platform made of packing boxes and shouted for quiet. "Well, boys," he cried, "—and fair ladies, we got us a new town here, but it ain't got no name. It jest hollers out for one, too. Anybody got any idees?"

Men began muttering, until finally one called out, "How about Kentucky? That's where some of us hail from."

Dutch Frank shook his head while the men spoke among themselves again. "We got to satisfy the post office. It won't do, Billy," he called out. "There are too many Kentucks already. Nope, we got to have somethin' diff'runt."

"We could call it O'Neil after the man who found the silver lode!" someone cried.

"Let's name it after the mule who done all the work!" shouted a second man, while everyone except Jemmy roared with laughter.

"Well, why not?" I heard him mutter.

Mama held up her hand and I saw her blush at her own courage. "I have an idea," she said softly, when Dutch Frank pointed at her and motioned for silence. "Did anyone ever live here before silver was discovered?"

"Sure," Dutch Frank boomed. "A Colonel Wallace used to homestead somewhere around these parts."

"Well, if he was here first, why not name the town Wallace?" she suggested. "He may not have found the lode, but he does deserve some sort of honor."

"Let's call it O'Neil," I whispered, tugging at Mama. But I was outvoted, for the miners reacted to her proposal by tossing their hats up in the air and cheering her.

"Well," Luke Gordon commented, as he escorted the three of us back to our tents, "you have named a town, Mrs. Scott. I'm sure there aren't many places named Wallace in the country."

"It certainly was done with dispatch," Mama approved, for she always preferred things to be done in an efficient manner.

Mama was quite pleased with herself for having named the town, and she asked Mr. Gordon in for a cup of coffee.

Helga sighed when we came in, and put down the shotgun. "I never know if it's goin' to be that Arrowsmith Farr varmint or not," she said.

"I don't think he's around here. At least he'd better

141

not be," Luke Gordon said grimly, sitting down at one of the tables near the warm cookstove. "He knows better than to come up here. He's a real bad one."

"What makes him act as he does?" asked Mama. "What do you know about him?" She came up to him with our best cup in one hand and the coffeepot in the other.

Luke Gordon poured sugar into his coffee. Finally he said, "Farr is a strange one. Nobody knows much about him. He showed up in Eagle City first with a string of pack mules, which he starved and beat pretty bad all the time. Then after you folks met him and had that run-in with him at Cataldo Flats, he sold his mules, and nobody knows what he does for a livin' now. Of course, there are men hereabouts that say Farr is a stage robber and a real desperado, but it can't be proved for a fact. There was a robbery on the stage that goes from Rathdrum to Fort Sherman jest before you folks come up here. They caught one of the bandits, but the other got clean away. 'Course with a mask on his face, it was hard to tell, but people on that stage swear that he looked like Farr, and talked jest like him too. That is, most of 'em said so—those that wasn't killed by the bandits."

Mama gasped and put her hand over her mouth.

"I guess he really hates us, doesn't he?" I asked.

"Well," Luke Gordon said, "you made a jackass out of him at Cataldo Flats, when a lady held a gun on him, and you did it agin when your boy's mule chased him through Eagle, and you really done it when you showed him up wrong about a Chinaman bein' in your tent. He'll do anything to get even with you for havin' him run out of the camp. Both times he meddled with you folks, you booted him right in his pride, where it hurts him most."

"You don't paint a very pretty picture for the future," Mama remarked quietly.

"I don't want to scare you none, Mrs. Scott," Mr. Gordon hastened to add, "but you better know the facts. We'll all try to look out for you, and if Farr comes up here and we get an eyeful of him, we'll run him out of Wallace too, you bet."

Mama smiled at this, went back for the second-best cup for herself, and sat down opposite Mr. Gordon. "Do have another cup of coffee, Mr. Gordon," she said, in a voice I'd never heard her use before.

Helga motioned to Jemmy and me to follow her, so we left the restaurant tent for our own. Helga pinched my cheek, while she whispered, "Well, little lady, your maw is makin' real progress these days, in more ways than one."

We started the restaurant just as quickly as we could, and no one grumbled because our bill of fare wasn't as nice or because our prices were a little higher than they had been in Eagle City. They all seemed to understand and be grateful that we had opened up while they were trying to get settled too.

In a few days it was hard to tell Wallace from the tent city we had just left. Everything, from the sawmill to the dance halls, was going full steam. It was amazing how quickly everything was done.

On the Monday after we came to Wallace we took the day off, and the four of us started for the Lucky Clover. Mama wasn't eager to go, but she said she'd grin and bear it, so she put on her oldest clothes and heaviest shoes and came along. Helga and Jemmy lashed supplies for O'Neil on Timothy Clover's back, guessing what he'd need. Then we left.

We went through Wallace along the pine-dotted gulch, and finally came to the Lucky Clover trail.

"Good heavens!" Mama exclaimed, as we climbed up to where O'Neil's markers stood among huckleberry bushes and rocks. "Is this a mine?"

"Not yet," Helga answered, "but it will be pretty soon, I bet."

Mama shook her head vigorously, and I agreed with her. There was nothing there at all but a few split-apart outcroppings of rock, which told us O'Neil had been using giant powder.

As we came up to his little tent, O'Neil hurried to meet us, taking off his battered hat and bowing low. "Welcome, ladies, to the Lucky Clover," he called out.

Mama sniffed and kept silent. Just then Nehemiah Spotted Horse stepped from behind O'Neil's tent, holding a miner's pick in his hand. He glanced at us, grunted, and walked off behind some bushes, and a moment later we heard the sound of his pick striking against rock.

"So Nehemiah come up here to you," Helga commented, "that's jest what the little lady said he'd do."

"He is my esteemed helper, and the first man to be on the payroll of the Lucky Clover," explained O'Neil. "And what do you think of the mine, ladies?"

"I don't see any mine!" Jemmy exploded.

O'Neil winked at my brother. "Just have a little patience, me boy. The assay report came back to me the other day. I did not miscalculate the wealth of the Lucky Clover. A mining engineer inspected it early today; the veins are rich. He tells me, dear friends, that the Lucky Clover may well be the richest silver mine this country has ever seen. We shall get a good price for her indeed. And now we are beginning to sink our shaft and carve out our first tunnel."

"That's all very fine to know," Mama put in, "but is Nehemiah Spotted Horse coming back to Wallace with us or not? We may be wealthy, but we still have to maintain our restaurant."

O'Neil looked up at the sky while he fingered his

red, curling mustache. "It's a very strange thing, but Nehemiah has intimated strongly to me that he would prefer not to go back to work for you. He said a most peculiar thing."

Helga snapped, "What was that, little man?"

"He said it was too dangerous working for you dear ladies. You didn't shoot at him, Helga, my love, did you? What do you suppose he meant?"

O'Neil fixed us all with his eye and smiled faintly. It was clear that he'd been told all about the trouble we'd had back in Eagle City with the Chinese man and Farr.

Helga looked at Mama as innocently as a baby would. "Mrs.," she said, "you got any idee why Nehemiah thinks it's dangerous to be around folks like us?"

"Well, he is different," O'Neil remarked. "I guess we'll never know what got into Nehemiah."

That conversation was dropped, and I, for one, was pleased. I had wondered more than a little how O'Neil would take the news. I had no idea how he felt about Chinese, but he must have approved of what we did, for he never brought up the subject again. Sometime later Jemmy heard from Nehemiah, himself, that he had taken Wang Erh out by boat as far as he could go on the Coeur d'Alene River, and then had carried him to where he knew there were other boats and had smuggled him into Fort Sherman. Wang Erh's wound was taken care of at the army post, and there Nehemiah had left him. He had waited among the Indians at Cataldo Flats until he heard something of O'Neil's whereabouts, and then he had come to the Lucky Clover mine to rejoin his old friend. Nehemiah Spotted Horse had never had any intention of coming back to fill the wood boxes at Scott and Storkersen's in Eagle City.

The autumn passed quickly for us, as time always does when you are busy. A wagon road was built to Wallace in a very short time, and this solved the sowbelly-and-beans problem quite nicely, for the store shelves were well stocked. Mama hired a man to get venison and elk for us several times a week, and during the evenings Helga hurried to preserve meat and vegetables for the winter, boiling away great tubs of food late into the night.

As for O'Neil O'Neil and Nehemiah Spotted Horse, they not only worked on their mine shaft, but they also built a little wooden shack to live in. It wasn't much to look at, for they'd thrown it up in a hurry, but it was better than the little tent in winter weather.

We were all in a rush. Helga didn't like the look of the October weather. She said that she could foretell the weather, and warned that we were going to have a hard winter. It seemed as if she was right.

The sky got dark-gray one afternoon, far darker than the gray of any Palouse dust storm, and by evening it had begun to snow.

Helga went outside, looking up at the sky as the dry snow hit her stingingly in the face. "It's jest as I said it was goin' to be," she commented with a frown. "Here it is, not the middle of the month yet, and it's goin' to be danged near a blizzard today, I bet. We got to get up to O'Neil jest as soon as we can get through the drifts, and see to it that the little man don't starve to death. Everybody up in the hills is goin' to be stayin' there for some time until the snow settles itself down. I sure don't like that steep gully he's got his shack holed up in. I tried to tell him diff'runt, but he wouldn' pay me no mind. Jest like a man, ain't it?"

"Why's that?" I asked. "O'Neil O'Neil and Nehemiah will get by better than they did in that little tent."

"I'm scared of a big snow," she replied. "It won't be bad for us. We're down here on flat ground in our tents. I'm scared that the snow might come loose and come tearin' right down on that puny little wood shack up there."

"You mean an avalanche!" I exclaimed.

"I sure do. They're real bad things. I've heard tell about the kind of things they do in mountain country like this. Even a man sneezin' or blowin' his nose can set the things off."

"I've read about avalanches in places like Switzerland, but that sort of thing doesn't happen here. This isn't the Alps," I scoffed.

"Don't you argue with me. I know what I'm sayin' better'n you do, and I'm worried." Helga paused thoughtfully for a moment and then went on. "We better go up there jest as soon as we can get out of here, and take a look and see if things is goin' along all right."

But we didn't get to go anywhere for three or four days. It snowed all that night and all of the next day. By the time we looked out of our snug tent one bright cold morning, the snow was piled up to our waists, and we had an unhappy hour shoveling it away from the door of the restaurant, so our customers could eat breakfast.

"There's got to be crust over this snow before we can do much walkin' around," said Helga. "It ain't goin' to be fun climbin' way up to the Lucky Clover, even if there is a good thick crust. We got to wait till there's a few more days of sunshine, and then we'll head out."

We waited, and while we waited Helga worriedly questioned everyone who came into our restaurant about the drifts up in the canyons. She did not seem any happier when she heard what she had suspected—that the snow was much deeper and softer there. She scowled when Luke Gordon told her that some canyons had had ten feet of drifts blown down into them by the wind before the storm had let up.

The morning of the fourth day Helga approached Mama, suggesting that we try to make it up to the Lucky Clover. Mama flung up her hands in horror at the idea, and refused to go anywhere near the mine, and at first she didn't want Jemmy or me to go either.

"It'll do 'em good to get out and shake their legs," Helga told her. "And they'll be so tuckered out when they get home, there won't be a peep out of 'em for a week."

"Well," Mama commented, weakening, "thank the Lord for small mercies. You'd better keep bundled up, Ann Katherine. And Jemmy, don't get your feet wet."

We whooped and hollered a bit, running to get our boots and heaviest clothes, and then helped Helga put a pack of dry supplies on her back. She had not allowed Jemmy to take Timothy Clover, saying that the mule would flounder around too much in the snow and get tired out. She added that he might catch cold, too, so Jemmy decided at once that this would never do. Timothy stayed behind in Wallace, with Mama to keep him company while Jemmy was gone.

The gulch certainly looked different under its coat of snow. The sky was a hard blue, with the sun brighter than I had ever seen it in Portland. It shone on the crusted-over whiteness with tiny sharp points of light. Your eyes hurt just looking around that white world, and now and then I looked up at the sides of the gulch at the dark green of the pines to help my eyes out. There was no one around working claims that day. We saw smoke coming from many tents along the trails and on the hills, but we didn't see any other people.

"It's too cold for anyone to be doin' any work with his hands today," commented Helga, trudging along through the snow on a path that someone had shoveled off a day or two before. Snow had drifted over the path, and it crunched like candy-making sugar under our boots. We walked single file to where the trail ended and the turnoff came for the Lucky Clover. The snow was about up to Helga's knees there, and evidently had not been brushed away or trampled down at all.

"It looks as if O'Neil and Spotted Horse haven't had no visitors, and it looks as if they haven't come down either," Helga said, beginning to wade through the snow, tramping it down as she went along.

We followed the path Helga made for about a hundred feet, until she plumped herself down on the snow and panted. "See if you two can't walk on the crust. You're light as a couple of feathers," she said. "This trail breakin' is too hard for a fat old Swede woman like me."

I stared at Helga. Her face was as red as a robin's breast, while her hair under a heavy wool scarf was damp with perspiration. It was the first time I had ever known her to be tired.

"Don't jest stand there gawkin'; see if you can get movin' on the crust!"

Obediently Jemmy and I walked very carefully for a few feet on the thick-frozen, yellowish-white snow layer. We did not fall through, and in a moment Jemmy was running.

"You come back here, sonny," Helga called to him. "You save all that energy you have. You and your sister are goin' to have to go on to the Lucky Clover alone and see how things are up there. You tell O'Neil to send Nehemiah down to break a trail, and then I'll come on up with his supplies and grub."

We were very proud to think that Helga trusted us enough to send us off alone. We hurried over the snow, breaking through now and then, and often grabbing bushes and branches of trees to help us on our way. At last we reached the ravine, and stood there for a while catching our breath and staring at O'Neil's shack, which was half-covered with snow. The shack had been built close up to a steep hill, and a huge drift had built up above it and behind it. The cabin looked small and rickety next to all that snow.

No one was in sight, although there was smoke coming from the tin chimney. Jemmy cupped his hands to his mouth to call, but I caught his arm and stopped him shaking my head. I felt a sudden chill, which I didn't understand, and at the same time I remembered Helga's warning about the overhanging snow. "We'll go up to the cabin and knock," I told Jemmy. "O'Neil and Nehemiah might be asleep."

"At noon?" Jemmy asked in scorn.

I didn't bother to answer him. Instead, I started off over the drifts, stopping at the door for Jemmy to catch up with me. A place had recently been shoveled off, so the door could be opened, and I knew by this that someone was inside. I lifted my hand to rap, but the door was pulled open so suddenly that I almost knocked on a man's chest.

It was Arrowsmith Farr.

CHAPTER 10

Arrowsmith Farr

I started to step back, but instead fell backwards onto a drift, knocking Jemmy down behind me. Before either of us could make another move, Arrowsmith Farr grabbed each of us by the back of the collar and flung us into the cabin, where we fell flat on the dirt floor.

It all happened so fast and was such a surprise that I didn't have time to be frightened. That feeling came, though, the minute Farr slammed the door shut, bolted it, and turned to face us. Then I realized that we were alone in O'Neil's cabin with our enemy.

"Git up, you brats," he snarled at us.

Jemmy and I stared at Farr, dirty and unshaven, his strawlike hair more messed up than ever above his lead-colored face and wild-looking eyes. His clothes were dirty and tattered, with the exception of a heavy corduroy coat, which I recognized as belonging to O'Neil O'Neil.

155

"Git up, I told you. Git up right now, or I'll git you up!"

Jemmy and I got to our feet and stood watching Farr carefully, the way a little animal watches a big hungry one. My teeth wanted to chatter, but I kept them tightly closed. I felt that if either of us showed fear in front of this man, we would be in even more danger.

"What did you do with Nehemiah Spotted Horse and O'Neil O'Neil?" Jemmy asked him, braver than I ever could have been. He stood there scowling at Farr, with his hands in his pockets and his legs spread apart, all ready to fight.

Farr grinned his ugly grin, passed his finger over his throat, and made a noise with his tongue. "I done in both the Indian and the little galoot," he told us.

"I don't believe you for one minute," said I, finding some courage at last. "I don't think you've done a single thing to Nehemiah and O'Neil."

"That's right," Jemmy taunted him. "Nehemiah Spotted Horse could break you right in two with one hand."

Arrowsmith Farr shrugged, and walked across the cabin floor, lifted the lid on the little iron stove, and stirred up the fire. He didn't answer.

"How did you get up here anyhow?" Jemmy asked him. "You're trespassin' on our claim."

Farr turned and glared at Jemmy. "I come down

over the hills behind this shack, but it ain't none of your business, any more than it's your claim."

"But it *is* our mine. The Lucky Clover belongs to O'Neil, Helga, Mama, and Jemmy and me," I insisted, getting more angry than frightened.

Once more Farr shrugged, and stooped to put some sticks in the stove. "Not for long it ain't goin' to belong to you folks. It's goin' to be mine," he stated.

"Well, just how do you plan getting the Lucky Clover?" flared Jemmy.

"You'll jest plain up and give it to me," said Farr, coming over closer to us and seating himself in O'Neil's only chair.

"Oh no, we won't!"

"You brats set down right over on that bunk, and we'll have us a nice little talk," he ordered. "Now you do like I say." As he said this, he took out his mean-looking skinning knife and began to play with it.

I got Jemmy by the coat sleeve, dragging him over to one of the two bunks that O'Neil had built against the walls of the cabin. "Let's humor him, Jemmy," I whispered. "I don't think he's right in the head."

"He's not going to get our claim," Jemmy whispered back fiercely, but he said no more when Farr's knife suddenly came whistling through the air and landed, quivering, in the wall only a few inches from Jemmy's left ear.

157

"There won't be no talkin' between the two of ya," Farr thundered. "You're my pris'ners, and when I talk, you keep shet up. D'ya hear me?"

We nodded, and were as silent as scared mice, while Farr got up and came over to us to pry out his knife. He passed the blade only a fraction of an inch from Jemmy's nose, as if he was going to slice it off, and I was proud that Jemmy didn't flinch.

"Next time I have to throw this here sticker I won't miss," he warned us, sitting down again. "I mean business, and I want you to know that. I figgered this whole thing out a long time ago, when I first heard that you had struck it rich. Pretty smart, ain't cha? But you ain't no smarter than Arrowsmith Farr. You made me out to look purty dumb a coupl'a times, but you've had all the licks you're gonna git. I'm gonna have the last laugh when you all give me bills of sale for this here claim."

"I don't think you could make us do that," I said slowly. "We would never sell the Lucky Clover to you in a million years."

Farr leaned forward and sneered at me. "My luck's been changin' in the last few hours. First I come up here and got me this nice warm shack, and then, jest like little jack rabbits, you march up and give me my ace cards. Mebbe I only had two kings before, but now I got me two aces, and I sure mean to use 'em. Now you brats keep shet up while I do some thinkin'. I got to figger the best way to play my aces."

The man turned his head away from us, and looked hard out the one window, as he thought it over. It certainly couldn't be that he was seeing anything out there, for the window was covered by a high drift of snow.

My mind raced. Where were Nehemiah and O'Neil? I didn't believe that Farr had really killed them. There were no signs of a fight in O'Neil's neat little cabin. But still, he had referred to having two kings in his hand. He must have meant O'Neil and Nehemiah Spotted Horse when he said that. But where were they? Had Farr really killed them and perhaps buried them under the snow? I asked myself. How long had he been in O'Neil's cabin—hours, days perhaps?

Suddenly Farr interrupted my sad thoughts by snapping his fingers. "I got it now," he said laughing. "You brats are goin' to come in real handy. I'm goin' to send the little gal down to Wallace to git that old mud hen of a female and her skinny maw to sign over their shares of this here mine to me. And if they don't, sonny here—who's goin' to stay behind to keep me from bein' lonesome—is goin' to be in real bad trouble."

"No, I'm not going to do any such thing," I announced. "Mama and Miss Storkersen wouldn't sign over anything to you—I know that. Anyhow, Mama really doesn't own a quarter of the mine. Jemmy and I own it."

Arrowsmith Farr laughed nastily. "Don't you go gettin' idees that your maw can't sign for you. You two are jest a pair of brats. You ain't of age, and you don't own nothin'."

I felt Jemmy swell up with anger beside me, but he wisely held his tongue.

"You git started, and you tell your maw jest what I told you," Farr warned me. "And no funny business neither, if you want to see your brother in one piece agin."

I got up to go, turning my back for a second on Farr. I pretended to fix my neck scarf, but actually I was silently moving my lips to say "Helga" to Jemmy. I knew that Farr didn't know how close she was to the cabin. Helga would know what to do, if anyone would. Perhaps we could round up O'Neil and Nehemiah, and attack. Jemmy's eyes lit up, showing me he understood that I was going to get Helga.

Then I turned around once more and started to pass Arrowsmith Farr. I looked at him as icily as I could, but he only laughed and then, without warning, grabbed my arm and pinched it as hard as he could. I almost cried out with the sudden sharp pain, but I held it back and didn't shame myself in his eyes or, more important, in Jemmy's.

"Keep your hands off me, if you please," I said, amazed at how much I sounded like Mama. "I may have to do your dirty work, but I do not have to put up with anything more."

Farr slapped his thighs with laughter. "Like cat, like kitten, they tell me," he crowed. And then he imitated my voice, "Do keep your hands to yourself, you dirty man."

I jerked away, but he suddenly caught me and dragged me back, clapping a bad-smelling hand over my mouth. "Keep shet up, both you brats," Farr ordered. "There's somebody comin' here. It must be them two kings I was talkin' about."

Farr flung me away from him, and I stumbled back to the bunk, where Jemmy still sat with round eyes. Then Farr gestured once more at us with his knife. "If you open your faces jest one time, I'll let you have this."

We sat still and frozen with fear once again, while Farr listened at the door. He had ears like a fox, for he had heard someone coming long before we did. We could hear the crunch of snow underfoot now, as someone approached the cabin. I wondered if it could be Helga, who had grown tired of waiting for Nehemiah to break a trail down to her. Did Helga have her derringer along? But then Farr knew all about her carrying a gun. Anyway, it must be Nehemiah Spotted Horse or O'Neil O'Neil, for Arrowsmith Farr had mentioned kings. Was he going to kill them when they came in?

Farr moved back of the door, taking a pistol from his belt. He stood there motionless, waiting, just as Jemmy and I did. I wanted to cry out to warn them, but Farr's knife lay within easy reach of his hand. I did not know if I could call to Nehemiah and O'Neil in time, anyhow. They were nearly at the door now, and would be opening it at any moment.

Arrowsmith Farr motioned to Jemmy to come over to him, and then whispered to my brother. Jemmy stepped away, shaking his head, but Farr drew back his hand as if to hit him. Slowly Jemmy unbolted the door and opened it, standing in the entrance, a small black figure against the white of the snow outside.

There, only a few feet in front of him, stood O'Neil and Nehemiah Spotted Horse, stamping their feet and shaking from their hats the snow that had fallen on them from the eaves of the shack.

"Well, this is indeed a most pleasant surprise," announced O'Neil, "to find such a handsome, distinguished, and wealthy visitor at our humble abode. Would that we knew you were arriving, me boy. We would have been here to greet you and not be toiling in the cold, silvery bowels of the Lucky Clover, as we have been all morning long." Nehemiah Spotted Horse nodded to Jemmy as O'Neil went on. "Well lad, do not block the doorway. Let us in to savor the warmth of the fire, which I see you have kept alive and glowing for us."

Jemmy did not move or speak, but stood blocking the door, staring at the two men.

"Lad, are you well?" asked O'Neil. "Where is that fine woman, Miss Storkersen, and where is your charming sister?" Then O'Neil spied me, and spoke across Jemmy's head. "Ah, there you are, little lady!" he called out, brushing by Jemmy gently, with Nehemiah following him.

I covered my eyes with my hands as they came in, but not before I saw Arrowsmith Farr step out from behind the door, jerk Jemmy inside, and strike Nehemiah Spotted Horse on the head with the barrel of his pistol. He pressed O'Neil hard against the wall with the gun to his chest, while Nehemiah slumped heavily to the floor.

"That takes care of the big Siwash," said Farr. "And now my hand's really ready to play, ain't it?"

"What do you want of us?" O'Neil asked in a strange voice. He stared down at Nehemiah and then at Farr's pistol, as if he couldn't believe in what had just happened.

"I been hearin' as how you lately got to be a real

big man, a mineowner and all. I bet you got a good hunk of cash stowed around this place somewheres, and I think you'll tell me where it is. Then you'll make me the owner of your share of this here claim jest to keep me in a good nature."

O'Neil shook his head, answering Farr coldly. "I have no cash, as you term it, concealed on these premises. Nehemiah Spotted Horse and I are developing the claim alone, without any real capital yet. Furthermore, I do not believe that anything I could possibly do would improve your naturally vile nature."

Farr grinned, and struck O'Neil smartly across the face with his big hand. "I reckon you could be tellin' the truth about the cash," he said. "This here cabin sure ain't no palace by a long sight. But we ain't settled nothin' about givin' me the claim. I think you'd better give me a bill of sale for your part here and now, mister."

O'Neil drew himself up to his full height, until, strangely enough, he looked tall. "I won't be giving you any bill of sale for something you haven't bought," he announced.

"We'll see about that," Farr cried, hitting him again. "You git on over there to that table, and you write me out a bill of sale like I told you to do."

"No," said O'Neil calmly, "I won't do it. I've prospected for thirty years, and no highbinder is

164

going to make me give up my first strike in all that time."

"I could shoot you," said Farr, smiling.

"That wouldn't get you the Lucky Clover!"

"Well, there's other ways then," Arrowsmith Farr went on. "D'ya notice that I've got the two brats here?"

Jemmy started to say something, but Farr stopped him. "You shet up, sonny," he thundered, "or I'll come over there and shet your mouth for you."

"Keep quiet, Jemmy," I told my brother. "He means what he says."

"I sure do," Farr approved my words. "I mean jest what I say. Now that I got the problem under control, I'm goin' to like every minute of it."

He turned his face toward O'Neil, and motioned at him with his pistol. "I got six bullets, mister," I heard him say. "I'm a purty good shot, so it'll only take one apiece for you, the brats, and the Siwash here. Now you git over to that table and write like I told you."

O'Neil looked at us and shook his head. He walked slowly to his rickety little wooden table and sat down, Farr following him, pistol in hand.

"You write me out a bill of sale," Farr ordered, "and everything will be fine for all you folks. I git my bill of sale from you, O'Neil, and the little gal here gets 'em from her maw and that fat old Swede mud hen. Then I sees to it that everything comes out all right for everybody. You jest wait and see."

O'Neil O'Neil took up a sheet of paper, which was already lying on the table, and began to write, while Farr watched him. When O'Neil had finished, the other man grabbed the paper and looked at it, chuckling. For a while I had hoped that Farr couldn't read and that O'Neil could trick him, but it seemed that he could, for he read it aloud, stumbling over a word here and there. Then he laughed once more, and while we looked on he swiftly tied up O'Neil and the still unconscious Nehemiah Spotted Horse, and rolled them like sacks of wheat across the floor and under the wall bunks.

"Now, gal," Farr said to me, "you git goin' on down to Wallace, and do what I told you to do. And mind ya now—no funny business."

"Bring back the United States marshal, Ann Katie!" Jemmy yelled at me, as Farr grabbed me by the collar again and pushed me toward the door, my feet barely touching the floor.

The last thing I saw before Farr shut the door in my face was Jemmy covering his head with his arms and Farr walking across the cabin floor toward him, pistol in hand. Then as I stood undecided in front of the door, I heard Jemmy cry out sharply twice, and I began to cry.

CHAPTER 11

Avalanche

I began my sad trip back down the snow-covered trail. Right then I was sure that I would never again see Jemmy, O'Neil O'Neil, or Nehemiah Spotted Horse alive. Arrowsmith Farr would kill them when he received the bills of sale for the Lucky Clover. There would be no witnesses to his claims, and I knew there would be plenty of men nearly as wicked as he, who would buy his mine without asking how he got it. He could shoot me and anyone else with me when I came back up to the shack, and there wouldn't be anyone the wiser for it. He could bury us under the heavy snow, and we wouldn't be found by any searchers until April at the earliest. At all costs, I had to keep Mama and Helga from coming back with me, and I didn't dare tell Luke Gordon or Dutch or any of our other friends in Wallace. Arrowsmith Farr would kill Jemmy, O'Neil, and Nehemiah at once if strangers came up to the claim.

So I stumbled along, my eyes filled with tears, and almost ran into Helga, who was puffing her way up the trail toward the rise in front of O'Neil's cabin.

"Where in the blue blazes have you been?" she demanded of me.

Then she saw that I was crying—and I went at it all the harder now that I was with her and knew I didn't have to bear the trouble all alone.

"Why are you bawlin', honey?" she asked in a kinder tone of voice. "You sure been gone up there a long time."

I flung my arms around Helga and buried my face against her chest. "Oh, Helga," I sobbed out, "Arrowsmith Farr's up there, and he's got Jemmy and O'Neil and Nehemiah as his prisoners. He wants the Lucky Clover. He made O'Neil give him a bill of sale, and he made me come down to get the other ones from you and Mama."

"Why, that's plumb crazy!" Helga stated, shaking her head. "Is this a joke you, O'Neil, and sonny are playin' on me?"

"It's not a joke," I cried, sniffling back more tears. "It's all true. He's got O'Neil and Nehemiah tied up and stuffed away under the bunks, and he's holding them and Jemmy, just in case I don't come back with what he wants. I think he plans to shoot all of us once he gets the Lucky Clover."

Helga lifted my chin and looked into my face for a moment. "I believe you," she said finally. "It's too silly not to be true. That Farr man must be out of his head."

"I think he might be," I responded. "But he's dangerous just the same. He thinks he can get away with it, and I think he can too."

"We'll see about that," Helga announced grimly. "We ain't goin' back to Wallace as meek as little sheared lambs. Not while I got my derringer handy."

"No, Helga," I cried, "Farr has a big pistol. We have to do what he says."

"Well, mebbe that's so, but we're sure gonna go back up there and take a good look around! Could Farr see us if we didn't go up to the shack door?"

"No, there's only the one window, and it's covered over with snow," said I.

"Well, come along, and we'll see what there is to see. Mebbe we can put our heads together and figger some way to get them outa there."

I shook my head, but gave in to Helga's words. She was older and wiser than I was, and perhaps there was something that the two of us could do, without going back to Wallace and terrifying Mama.

Helga set her lips in a firm line and started off up the trail again, pushing and stamping the ever deeper snow away in front of her. As for me, I walked on the crust once more. We went on in silence for a short time until we came out at the top of the rise that looked down on O'Neil's place.

It looked just the same, and was so peaceful that you'd never believe what lay inside or what had just happened there. The same little steady stream of smoke came out of the tin chimney, gray-blue against the overhang of snow.

"Well," said Helga, "whatever that Farr varmint is doin' to 'em, he ain't freezin' 'em to death. Now you jest keep quiet for a spell, while I do some heavy thinkin'."

I sighed, and leaned against a snowdrift. I was too tired to think any more, so I stared, without a thought in my head, at the mass of snow built up behind the cabin. And as I was gazing at the snow and waiting for Helga to have an idea, Jemmy took things in his own hands.

The door of the shack burst open, and my brother came hurtling out, skipping over the snow crust faster than I'd ever known he could move. Arrowsmith Farr came pounding hot on Jemmy's heels for perhaps ten feet, and then began to flounder in the snow, snarling, cursing, and spitting like an angry cougar.

"You stay here," ordered Helga, pushing me down on the cold white surface, and she began to plow her way toward Jemmy, who was still running. "Over here, sonny!" she called out, as I lost my breath with fright. "Get over here as fast as you can!"

In a flash, Jemmy saw her and changed his course toward us. Farr saw us, too, and stopped thrashing about. He grinned and, lifting the heavy pistol he had in his hand, he drew on Jemmy's back. I held back a scream. He fired, but a second before he fired, Helga did too, shooting her little derringer at him. Helga's tiny gun couldn't possibly have carried the distance to hit Arrowsmith Farr, but it was so unexpected that it upset his aim. He missed Jemmy, who came bounding up to Helga and into her arms.

"We got to get out of here fast," she yelled. "My derringer ain't no match for a forty-four pistol. Run, you two!"

I scrambled to my feet just in time to see Farr raise his gun again, but we stood so close together that I couldn't tell where he aimed or at which one of us.

"Get down!" Helga yelled at Jemmy and me. "Don't give him a big target. Keep down!"

We did as she ordered, and rapidly four bullets whistled over our heads. We both began to cry, our faces buried in the snow.

"When he stops to reload, you run back off this here rise. You hear me?" Helga cried.

We kept down while we waited for Farr to use up all of his bullets, and while we waited we heard it— the most terrible roar imaginable.

"Oh, God!" Helga wailed, lifting her head a little and staring above the cabin. "It's comin'. God help all of us."

I looked up, too, and was terrified to see the entire side of the hill behind O'Neil's cabin start to move down toward us. Nothing in the world could ever have stopped it. Tons and tons of snow covered the cabin as we watched.

"The shack's going to be carried down the gully," Jemmy cried, "with Nehemiah and O'Neil inside it. They'll be crushed!"

"We got to get out of here right now," yelled Helga. "We got to save ourselves." And she reached down, pulling us to our feet. "That avalanche is still movin' down off the hill."

"What about O'Neil?" I screamed out over the roar.

Helga shook her head violently. "We got to get out of here," she repeated. "We can't do nothin' for O'Neil if we get buried too."

I turned to stare at the avalanche. It had lost some of its speed, but was still moving with a roar, full of rocks, boulders, and uprooted trees, across where the shack had last been seen.

"Look at Farr!" cried Jemmy. "The snow's goin' to get him!"

There stood Arrowsmith Farr, pushing through

172

the drifts as fast as he could. But he could not match the speed of the advancing wall of snow. Finally he stood up and flung his arms over his head. We heard one hoarse cry of terror from him just as the avalanche struck him.

I screamed and screamed. It was just like a nightmare—only I was wide awake.

Helga shook me and slapped me. "We got to get away from here. There's no time for carryin' on now."

She pushed me ahead of her, and all three of us began to move as fast as we could down the trail, Helga hurrying along in the path she had made, constantly looking back over her shoulder.

"Keep movin'!" she cried out to us. "Mebbe we can outrun the snow."

We slogged through the snow, until we reached the flat ground at the foot of the trail. Here we stopped and caught our breaths.

"Be quiet now!" Helga ordered. "Listen and see if you can still hear the roarin' sound."

We listened, standing still as statues, and we heard nothing at all.

"Well, I guess it's all over," said Helga, sitting down right in the middle of a drift. "I guess it's all done for now."

Jemmy sat down beside her and began to make such strange sounds that I couldn't tell if he was laughing or crying. He looked up at Helga and me and said in a choked-up voice, "That old bill of sale sure didn' do Arrowsmith Farr much good, did it?"

Helga nodded, agreeing with Jemmy. "Evil gets evil in return," she said, with tears in her eyes. "Mebbe Farr got what he deserved when the avalanche took him, but his evil doin' was the end of my feller O'Neil and Nehemiah Spotted Horse. Farr's shootin' brought the snow down. That's the hard part of it."

"Are you sure they're gone?" I asked her hopefully.

"I never did hear of anybody bein' covered by an avalanche and makin' it out alive," said Helga dully.

"But couldn't the shack have saved them?" I asked.

"The timbers would have fallen in on 'em. It'd be almost worse inside than outside. Even if they got caught in some sort of place where the wood didn' crush 'em, they'd suffocate without no air to breathe."

"Maybe they do have some air inside," Jemmy said hopefully. "I don't know what you're going to do now, but I'm running to Wallace to get men with shovels to dig out that cabin."

"You go on, sonny," Helga said, in the saddest way. "I'm goin' to stay right here. I ain't feelin' like doin' much more runnin' around today."

So Jemmy got to his feet and trudged off toward Wallace while Helga and I sat in the snow.

He came back before very long with a large crowd of miners, some carrying shovels, some with hand-saws, and others with long poles and teams of mules. Jemmy walked in front, leading Timothy Clover, and Mama came hurrying alongside the mule, Luke Gordon and Wallace's young doctor walking with her.

Luke Gordon spoke to Helga. "We hear from the boy here that there's been an avalanche up in the Lucky Clover gully."

"That's right," Helga answered tonelessly. "The whole shack was buried under the snow."

"Could you tell if it was crushed or not?" the doctor asked her.

"I don't see how it couldn't have been," she replied. "It must'a been nearly all the snow in the world that come down. The whole hillside went."

"Well, we'll dig right now," commented Luke Gordon, and I noticed that he touched Mama's shoulder and pointed to Helga. Mama promptly sat down beside Helga, putting her arm around her, and they both began to cry.

As for the men, they hastened to widen the trail with their shovels, and several of them went up ahead of the crowd as fast as they could go.

Jemmy and Timothy Clover followed along in the steps of the diggers, so I got up to go along with them, leaving Mama and Helga still sitting at the foot of the new trail. Mama didn't even try to stop me; I wasn't sure that she knew I had left her.

I caught up with Jemmy quickly, and the moment he saw me he said, "Ann Katie, they might be alive, you know."

I could only look at him and shake my head, but I couldn't really speak.

We climbed slowly up behind the snow shovelers, finding ourselves on the very spot where Farr had shot at us only a short while before. There wasn't a single thing in sight but the bare hillside and a vast sheet of snow, dotted with large boulders and snapped-off pine trees.

Luke Gordon took charge right away. "We're goin' to dig out that shack of O'Neil's, boys," he called, cupping his hands to his mouth. "It was up aginst the hill purty close, and that's where we'll start diggin'. Mebbe it got shoved out of place by the snow, but we got to start somewhere."

The men buzzed with talk as they began to dig their way through the high drifts. My, but it was hard work for them! They dug in shifts and got very red-faced, often coming back to rest on the dry, bare rock where Jemmy and I were sitting quietly.

"That snow's almost as bad as hard-rock minin' with a pick and drill," one of the men said to Jemmy. "But we'll git through before long, don't you fret none."

I stood up and looked. They weren't far from the cabin, if my memory was right. Then, as I watched, I heard Luke Gordon call out, but I couldn't hear his words because of the wind.

"He's found the shack, Jemmy," I told him. "I think he's found it. Let's go see!"

We rushed down the path, dodging shovelers, to see what Luke Gordon had found, but all we saw were a few boards of O'Neil's cabin.

Then Mr. Gordon himself caught us, and stopped us. "Oh no, you don't," he told us. "We've got some purty touchy diggin' to do now, so we sure don't need young'uns underfoot gettin' in the way. You scoot right back up to that rise, and sit down agin. We'll let you know soon enough what we find."

Jemmy and I were shocked. "We've got a right to be here," Jemmy cried. "O'Neil and Nehemiah are our best friends."

But Luke Gordon stood his ground and pushed us away from the diggers, who were quickly scrabbling away the snow from the boards, so the men and mules could get at what was left of the cabin.

We went back to our rock and waited, feeling very much left out of things. Finally a man came running back to us and shouted, "Have you kids seen the doc?"

"Somebody must be alive!" Jemmy cried out, pounding me on the back in his joy.

The doctor, who was a few yards away from us on the other side of the rise, dropped what he was doing and grabbed up his bag to run after the man who had called. He had been bandaging the foot of a miner who had stepped on a shovel while digging out the trail, and as the doctor left the miner called out after him, "Hey, doc, how about my foot?"

"I'll finish it later. There must be somebody alive in that shack," the doctor shouted, as he hurried past Jemmy and me.

Jemmy and I left Timothy Clover with a man who was resting on our rock, and circled around the gully in the snow, climbing on some large boulders that the avalanche had left bare. From there we could look down into the gully.

"See, Jemmy!" I cried, grabbing him by the coat sleeve. "See all the boards standing up? The cabin wasn't crushed. Look, they're using ropes and mules to pull off the boards that are flat."

"Luke Gordon and the doctor are crawlin' inside now," said Jemmy.

"They're going to get O'Neil and Nehemiah out, I bet," I yelled into Jemmy's ear.

We watched while Luke Gordon and the doctor came out, and were at once surrounded by a knot of men. Then several of the diggers went back inside the shell of the cabin, while others cast off ropes from the mules. Ever so slowly two of the men came out

178

of the ruins carrying something with them wrapped up in blankets. Then, even more slowly, others brought out another blanket-wrapped form.

"I guess they must be goners, or they wouldn't be all wrapped up like that," Jemmy said, tears beginning to run down his cheeks.

I gulped and watched as the doctor knelt down beside the men as they were laid on the snow. We both saw the doctor pull something out of his pocket, unscrew a top, and hold it out.

"They can't be goners, Jemmy," I hooted with happiness. "The doctor's giving them a lightnin' flash for sure. They can't even be too sick if he's doing that."

Jemmy hopped up and down. "Bein' under those bunks must have saved 'em," he cried out. "There must have been some air trapped in the shack. Let's go down and see how they are."

We leaped down off the rocks, at the risk of breaking our necks, but we didn't really care as we circled back along the gully and entered the shoveled-out path to the cabin. This time no one stopped us, so we practically skidded into O'Neil, who was sitting up in his blankets and reaching for the doctor's special medicine again.

He stared at Jemmy in amazement and poked Nehemiah Spotted Horse, who was also sitting up. "The lad's alive," O'Neil said softly. "The saints must have preserved him. That murdering devil Farr shot at him six times that I counted before the avalanche came."

"The shots weren't all at Jemmy," I cried. "Four of them were really fired at Helga and me, and only one shot was for Jemmy. The sixth shot you heard was from Helga's derringer."

"Great heaven!" said O'Neil. "Where is that pearl of a woman?"

"She's crying her eyes out over you at the foot of the trail," I replied. "She thinks you're a goner."

"Where's Farr?" asked Nehemiah, getting to his feet. "Like to fix him."

"The snow did your work for you, Nehemiah," I told him. "Arrowsmith Farr's buried under a couple of tons of snow, not fifteen feet from here."

"What?" exclaimed Luke Gordon. "Farr's up here, too? Nobody told us that."

"He sure is," said Jemmy, and there on the spot he told the whole story to Luke Gordon, the doctor, and the miners.

"Well, I'll be!" commented the doctor. "That's a real hair-raiser of a tale, son."

As Jemmy finished, Nehemiah Spotted Horse helped O'Neil to his feet. "We go down trail now," he said. "O'Neil go with Helga, and Nehemiah go back to reservation soon. Spotted Horse tired of white man and white-man ways."

Everyone laughed when Nehemiah said this, and the men brought forward two mules with ropes as halters around their necks.

"You're well enough, boys, to make it down the trail on mule power," was the doctor's statement. "You could probably walk it if you had to, but you didn't get a lot of air in that shack. You're sure lucky, though, that you were rolled under the bunks, instead of being out in the middle of the floor. Those bunks saved your lives, whether you know it or not."

"We know it," said O'Neil. "And the next house I build will be made of bricks."

The doctor shook his head, and gently slapped O'Neil's mule on the rump. A miner led it by the halter, and we all began to walk along the dug-out trail. I followed along as close as I could to O'Neil's mule, while Jemmy escorted Nehemiah, although it got pretty tight sometimes for us when we turned corners and the mules jammed us hard against the walls of snow.

O'Neil was tired and pale, but on the way up out of the gully he asked me again and again how Helga was. He seemed almost pleased that she was so upset over him. He stopped his questions, though, when we reached the rise, and Luke Gordon and his party of diggers asked Jemmy and me where we'd last seen Arrowsmith Farr.

On that large field of snow it was almost impossible to tell them, but we finally pointed out a spot, about fifteen feet from the ruins of O'Neil's cabin, which could have been the place. When we started down the trail toward level country, some miners had already slowly begun to shovel a path.

CHAPTER 12

Everything Ends Merrily

Oh what a reunion we all had down at the flats!

Helga took one look up at the trail, saw O'Neil O'Neil coming, and gave out the loudest shriek I ever heard. She leaped up, hiking her skirt up over her six flannel petticoats, and ran over to O'Neil and hauled him off his mule.

"We'll git hitched jest as soon as you say, little man," I heard her cry to him.

Then Mama dashed up to Luke Gordon, still crying, and shook his hand over and over again.

"What's she doing that for, Ann Katie?" Jemmy asked me suspiciously. "Mr. Gordon wasn't buried under any old avalanche."

"Well, he's a hero, I suppose," I answered. "After all he did get O'Neil and Nehemiah Spotted Horse out, didn't he?" But even as I said it, I didn't think that was the real answer.

In a few minutes Mama went over to O'Neil, and

I'll swear she seemed almost glad to see him. Then she spoke to Nehemiah, and laughed when he said that he'd had enough of white men and was going back to the reservation. I certainly did understand how he felt, what with all the trouble he'd gone through with O'Neil and the Scott family.

A few days later we all chipped in and gave Nehemiah a new suit of clothes, a big dollar pocket watch made of silver, and some money to jingle in his pockets. Then O'Neil presented him with a horse— a large rawboned dapple gray. This was by far his favorite gift. Nehemiah Spotted Horse got on it at once and, without even a good-by, rode out of Wallace and out of our lives.

Winter went on into spring—the snow finally melting away by the end of April. O'Neil went back up to the Lucky Clover, while Helga, Mama, Jemmy, and I kept on with our restaurant. Mama swore that as long as the claim remained unsold, we were going to keep on working, cooking food for the hungry silver miners, and putting gold eagles away in our little strongbox.

The railroad came in that spring, but they got a little ahead of themselves in their rush, and laid the tracks when there was still snow on the ground. When the snow and ice melted, so did the roadway, so the tracks buckled and had to be relaid. Everyone in Wallace thought this was very funny, and talked and laughed about it for a long time—even after the new railroad really came into Wallace.

With it came more and more people and a good deal of money. Mama swallowed her pride, and one Monday evening she and Helga took a large long-handled frying pan, and walked up and down the streets of Wallace, going from saloon to saloon asking for contributions for a church. I went with them, but much as I wanted to see what went on inside the swinging doors, I was ordered to stay outside. Mama looked quite pale when she went in and quite blush-pink when she came out, but she made it through all twelve of them. She and Helga did very well, too. In that one night they collected enough to buy lumber to build the church and to offer a preacher at Spokane Falls something for him to travel to Wallace for services every other Sunday. Mama even got promises from the lightning-flash drinkers to help build the church, and this pleased her even more than the gold pieces that showered down into her frying pan.

"You know," Helga commented thoughtfully, as we walked back to our tent, "I think me and O'Neil ought to use our new church first of all."

"Well, I do hold with getting married in a church," stated Mama primly, holding the covered frying pan, so it wouldn't clink about and attract desperadoes. Although Arrowsmith Farr's body had been found and he'd been buried in Wallace's new little cemetery, Mama still expected the worst from some of the town's citizens.

"Will you be getting married soon then?" I asked Helga.

"I got to take it up with O'Neil, and I got to have me a weddin' gown," she replied. "I'll traipse up to the gully and see what he says. The men swore they could put the church up in less'n a month. That don't give O'Neil and me a lot of time."

"I just love weddings," I murmured.

"But, Ann Katherine, you've never even been to one!" exclaimed Mama, staring down at me.

"It doesn't matter," said I. "I've read all about them."

Helga laughed, poked me with the point of her big black, man's umbrella, and winked. "Mebbe, there'll be more'n one hitchin' goin' on in the new church. Mebbe your maw'll be gettin' such idees too."

"Oh, fiddlesticks," said Mama. "Who would want to marry me?" But she said it with a smile.

In that month the church was built, just as planned. Everyone in Wallace, who was willing to get up early, came to the first services, and it was elegant—except that I did find it strange that the young new minister wore a gun under his vestments. You could see it sticking out of his pocket.

"That's sure a funny way to carry a gun," Jemmy whispered to me.

"Oh, he's not from Idaho Territory," I found myself saying. "He doesn't know how, I guess. He's from outside. Nobody carries a gun in his pocket. How would you ever get it out in time to use it?"

Mama said "Sh-h" at that moment, so we never did get to finish our talk, interesting though it was to both of us.

Luke Gordon walked us back after the services, coming in for a cup of coffee before we served Sunday dinner. We found O'Neil and Helga sitting opposite one another at one of the tables, waiting for us.

"I have a proposal for you, Mrs. Scott," said Luke Gordon, after his first sip of coffee.

Mama's eyes got very round, and her mouth opened wide. "Not in front of all these people!" she exclaimed.

"I want to make you an offer for the Lucky Clover," he said, and I got the impression that Mama was more than a little disappointed. "You know I've made money sellin' city lots, and I've done mighty well on the railroad and my freight lines, too. You say you want a buyer. Well, I got one for you— meanin' me! That's why I sent for you, O'Neil, to come down off the claim and talk business with me. As I understand it, O'Neil is half owner, Miss Storkersen here owns a quarter, and Mrs. Scott owns the other part of the mine."

"Ann Katie and I own it!" corrected Jemmy.

"Well, maybe your maw will let you sell to me," Luke Gordon went on, smiling at Jemmy. "I'll make you a good offer."

"I do believe that Dutch Frank and Montana Bellows were thinking of making us business overtures," said Mama a bit crossly. "I think we'd better let them have a chance, don't you?"

"I already outbid them," stated Mr. Gordon. "I know what they're fixin' to offer, and I can top it."

"Well, I never did hear of such highhandedness," Mama cried out.

"Now don't get so riled, Mrs. Scott," said Luke, lighting a cheroot without even asking permission. "It ain't that I really have my heart so set on the Lucky Clover, at that."

Mama looked quite surprised, as did Jemmy and I, but as she stared at Mr. Gordon angrily, we noticed Helga's big smile and O'Neil's winks.

Luke Gordon blew out a beautiful smoke ring. "Yep," he went on, "I got my sights set on somethin' real purty, and I'd like to think it would be goin' with the claim, if I offer to give you folks the capital to develop it. You see, I don't hanker after the whole mine. I'll put up the cash if you give me a quarter of it."

"Whose quarter?" demanded Mama, her blue eyes snapping with anger.

"Yours and you along with it!" declared Mr. Gordon, walking over to Mama. "It'd be known as the Gordon Quarter in these parts, I figure."

"Nope," said Helga, rising, "it'll be the Gordon Half. I don't need no quarter. I'll give Mrs. Scott my part of the Lucky Clover for a weddin' present when she hitches up with you, if she gives me her half of Scott and Storkersen's eatin' house."

"Why, I'm being disposed of as if I were a head of cabbage," cried Mama in disbelief. "Here I've just lost my half of the restaurant, all of the silver mine, and received the most peculiar proposal of marriage I've ever heard of—in front of four witnesses. And there's a mule, who's just stuck his head through the back tent flap and stolen the carrots that were to be in today's salad. I think I must be out of my mind, as I know all of you are."

With these words Mama put her hands over her ears and ran out of the tent.

"She didn't say 'no,' " said Luke Gordon hopefully.

"Now, my lad, you have to convince her," O'Neil

stated, shaking his head. "That wasn't the neatest, prettiest proposal I ever heard. You'd better put on quite a performance now."

"I sure will do that," Luke promised him.

All of Wallace enjoyed Mr. Gordon's courting of the Widow Scott. Boxes of gifts arrived daily— candy, bolts of silk and woolen cloth, great masses of wild flowers, and everything he could order from the stores in Wallace or in Spokane Falls. Still Mama would not speak to him, and she grew purple when she heard he was beginning to build a mansion at the edge of Wallace. The wagonloads of lumber for his house passed our tents, rumbling by every single day, and at least every other hour Luke Gordon himself came by, driving his fine new rig with the beautiful matched bay horses. He sent Mama a diamond ring, a gold watch, pearl earrings, and, to her horror, a gilded bathtub with claw feet. Mama promptly sent back all the jewelry and everything else he attempted to give her, but we wouldn't let her return the tub. We were sick and tired of bathing in our copper washtubs, so we clung to our glorious golden tub, while Mama stubbornly went on using the washtub.

Then he put up signs all around our tents, sticking them into the ground. They read, "Please!" "Speak to Me Again," and "Don't Be So Mule-headed!" This last sign made Mama so mad she was about to explode, for it mortified her to have our customers walk

190

through that forest of signs and then tease her when they came in to dine.

"I wouldn't marry that man if he was the last man on earth. He doesn't even know how to propose to a lady," she muttered day and night.

One afternoon I asked Helga what we should do. Things weren't getting any better. Mama was becoming thinner and paler, and was barely speaking to any of us. Mr. Gordon didn't look so well either. I was getting tired of the way things were going, and Jemmy and I had privately decided that we liked Mr. Gordon and wouldn't mind him at all for a stepfather.

"Why don't you and sonny take a hand in the romance?" asked Helga, holding up an apple pie and trimming off extra crust with a knife.

"How?" I asked.

"Show him how to pop the question right!"

"Where'll I find that out?" I asked again. "Nobody ever proposed to me yet, and O'Neil just came right out and asked you in front of me when he found the silver lode."

"Shucks, we ain't such fancy folks as your maw," commented Helga. "We don't have to have things done up so fine. You got some books, ain't cha? How is it done in stories?"

"Oh!" exclaimed I. "I'll look it up!"

I read everything we had, getting a few hints here and there, which I confided to Jemmy. "You fetch

191

him here like I told you," I warned him, giving him a list of instructions I'd written out for Mr. Gordon. "Be sure he gets here just at nine, and I'll have Mama all ready, not suspecting a thing."

I was very pleased with myself when Jemmy had gone with my message. I had written down everything Mr. Gordon would need to know. If he followed my instructions, all would be well.

He did follow them, too. Promptly at nine he appeared, his brown mustache waxed. He was wearing his best clothing; his watch chain and shoes were gleaming; his hair was parted and well combed and smelled delightfully of bay rum. In his left hand was his best hat and, in his right, a bouquet of roses, and most astonishing of all he wore no gun and holster. He looked wonderfully elegant. He stiffly followed Jemmy into the empty restaurant tent, where Mama was cleaning off the tables, and stopped before her.

Then he dropped to one knee on the dirt floor, offered her the flowers, and addressed her. "Madam, I have come to speak to you on a private matter of the utmost importance."

I caught Jemmy by the arm, dragging him out the back way, leaving Mama holding and smelling the pink roses. Luke Gordon was still on one knee, his free hand across his breast, while he rattled off the speech I had written for him.

"That's the silliest thing I ever saw anybody do," Jemmy snorted outside. "Is that how you got to propose to a girl? If that's so, I'll never get hitched."

"You just look through this hole in the canvas," I told him. "That's the kind of proposal ladies want, all right. That's what all the books tell about when the heroines say 'yes' and swoon."

Jemmy looked through the hole and turned back to me. "Mama's smiling at Mr. Gordon!" he exclaimed.

"What did I tell you?" said I, feeling very grown-up. "We now have a stepfather and half of the Lucky Clover, too. I think we've done pretty well up here."

"And I'll never have to wash another dirty pot or pan again," cried Jemmy. "Helga and O'Neil can have 'em all. Yippee!"

Of course, Mama accepted Mr. Gordon. How could she have refused such a proposal of marriage? They even set the date to be married the same day, early in the autumn, that O'Neil and Helga had chosen.

This left a whole six weeks for all the arrangements to take place. Mama, Helga, and I took the railroad to Spokane Falls to buy wedding clothes for all of us. I thought it was one of the nicest trips I had ever made, for we knew everyone on the train. They all wished Mama and Helga lots of luck, and though it isn't polite to congratulate the bride, Mama forgave them, saying she realized they meant well, even if they were ignorant.

Mama picked out a dress of light-blue silk to be made up by a Spokane Falls dressmaker, while Helga chose white silk, because she was getting married for the first time. Naturally both dresses were to be made in the very latest fashion, with most elegant bustles and dust ruffles at the hem. Helga had a crown of imitation orange blossoms and a veil, and although the gowns were to be sent from Spokane Falls to Wallace, she insisted on carrying this back with her in a hatbox.

I was outfitted, too. As a matter of fact, Mama let me have a dress made from pink sprigged surah, and, wonder of wonders, it had a bustle! I was to put my hair up and my skirts down on the day of the wedding, but I was not allowed, alas, to wear the false bangs I'd brought with me from Portland. We bought a new ready-made brown suit for Jemmy—one with long trousers, which he was really much too young to wear—and Helga bought a black wedding suit for O'Neil.

Mama, Helga, and I also bought new bonnets. Helga's was of shiny yellow straw, covered with white, red, and yellow roses, but awful as it was, she was delighted with it. Mama's and mine were just alike—white, with forget-me-nots on the brim.

Then we went back to Wallace, and waited for everything to arrive. We carried on with our business, while O'Neil and Jemmy worked at the mine. Mr. Gordon put a good deal of money into the Lucky Clover, so O'Neil was able to hire miners to work for us. Before long he had a foreman and a crew of powder-and-drill men and muckers at work in the shaft.

O'Neil could now come down into Wallace and supervise the building of what he called the "grandest and most glorious brick edifice Idaho Territory has ever feasted its sight upon." Privately I thought it couldn't compare with the beautiful wooden house Luke Gordon was building, with its gingerbread trim and its lovely cupolas and bay windows. O'Neil's house was large and expensive, but next to Mr. Gordon's fine four-story, canary yellow house, it looked square and squatty.

I did step inside the Lucky Clover one Sunday afternoon when no one but Jemmy, Timothy Clover, and I were up in the gully—superstition or no superstition against women. It certainly was nothing to see. "Hole in the ground" fitted it pretty well. You could see the veins of silver ore in the dark black-gray rock at the sides of the mine, but they didn't impress me very much. The richest mine in Idaho Territory was more interesting if you talked about it and didn't look into it.

Perhaps I shouldn't have done any peeking, though. The day of the wedding all of Wallace came pretty close to a bad end, because of Jemmy's and my being up in the gully alone.

"Hey, Ann Katie, look at that!" cried Jemmy, pointing to some boxes, labeled *Giant Powder*, which were stacked behind the ore cars at the entrance of the Lucky Clover. "Just think, that's what they put in firecrackers on the Fourth of July."

"You better not touch that stuff," said I. "It's dangerous if you don't know how to use it."

"Oh, it ain't so dangerous," Jemmy said, bending down and prying off the top of one box with a miner's pick he'd found on the tracks.

"I'll tell O'Neil," I warned him.

"Oh no, you won't," said my dear brother. "If you do, I'll tell him you went into the Lucky Clover. What do you think O'Neil will have to say about that? And, what's more, there's six boxes of powder here, so I'm carryin' two back with me to town. I got an idea of how to celebrate some weddings that are coming up."

"No, sir," said I. "You aren't taking any powder anywhere!"

"I'll tell!" he threatened again.

I thought for a moment. He meant it, and I knew it. O'Neil would be very angry if he knew I'd gone into the mine, silly as the superstition was. "All right," I said, "but you be careful with it."

And that's where I made my mistake, standing there doing nothing while Jemmy lashed the two boxes to Timothy Clover's back, covering them up with an old piece of canvas. We went back to Wallace, where he hid the boxes in some clumps of huckleberry bushes behind our tents, and then, in all the rushing around about the weddings, I forgot about the giant powder.

To Mama's shock, O'Neil had decided to have the biggest bang-up wedding Idaho Territory had ever known. Instead of sending out engraved invitations, he'd visited the local newspaper office and had them run off a couple of hundred posters, inviting people. Then he hired boys to go around nailing them to trees along the roads that led into Wallace. Anyone who read his posters and wanted to come was invited, for the last line read, "Nobody barred." He was going to add Luke Gordon's and Mama's names, too, but Mama begged him not to, so he finally gave in, after much arguing. Luke Gordon said he didn't care, and Helga and Jemmy thought it was great, but Mama and I were of a different opinion.

Oh my, after that, didn't the wedding gifts roll in, though! O'Neil and Helga received over 700 pounds of silverware—enough to set up the most elegant eating house in the West, said Helga. And enough to keep a whole staff of servants busy all year polishing it, said Mama.

Mama, of course, was given many gifts too, but they didn't compare in actual size with Helga's. But Mama seemed just as happy. Luke Gordon gave in most of the time to Mama's taste and ideas, but he did insist that the front hall in his nearly finished yellow house be paved with silver coins. Mama was shocked, but let him go ahead with it, telling me privately that she would cover it all with a red Brussels carpet the day we moved in.

The great day finally arrived. We dressed to the very teeth, Jemmy not even protesting when Mama washed his neck and ears. Needless to say, we had a family fight about Timothy Clover, for Jemmy wanted him to come to the wedding too, and had him all curried and groomed for the occasion. Mama stood firm, though, saying that the mule had run her life long enough. He might be given an extra carrot and lump of sugar to celebrate, but that was quite enough. Jemmy was sulking when we went into the new church, although I'm sure the Scott family never looked more handsome and fashionable than at that moment, for both Mama's gown and mine were copies of fashions by Worth of Paris, France, as the Spokane Falls seamstress had pointed out with great pride.

Helga and O'Neil swept up to the altar—Helga, large and happy in her white dress, orange blossoms, and veil, and O'Neil, small and happy in his new suit. Then Mama and Mr. Gordon took their places, and the new minister, who'd been asked by Mama not to wear his gun, married the two couples.

I cried. All the books I'd looked into on how to tell Luke Gordon the proper way to propose to Mama said that women guests were supposed to cry. It wasn't that the wedding or the church were so pretty, because they weren't really. The wedding was very short, and the inside of the church wasn't even painted yet. I cried, because I knew it was the proper thing to do, and all the other ladies, including the dance-hall and saloon girls, were also crying. It made me feel just as grown-up as my bustle and long skirts did.

After the wedding was over, we all went to Dutch Frank's for the celebration. It wasn't being run as a saloon. He and Montana Bellows had both closed for the day, and had gone together to give the brides and grooms a "send-off," as they called it. All 700 pounds of Helga's and O'Neil's silver were set up to be seen, and Mama's and Mr. Gordon's gifts were there too. Montana and Dutch Frank had put out a nice wedding lunch of roast venison, sour-dough bread, and everything else Wallace had to offer in the way of good food. They also had lots of champagne for the occasion, and Mama took a glass, which she choked on, to show she was a good sport. In honor of my long skirts, Helga let me have just one sip from her glass, and I decided right then and there that I didn't like it. It tasted like bottled gaslight to me.

Jemmy hadn't come inside with all of the wedding guests. I thought it was pretty strange that he wasn't hanging around the food the way he usually did, so I went to the big glass window of Dutch Frank's place and looked out, hoping to spy him.

While I looked, I couldn't help noticing how much Wallace had changed in the short time since it had been founded. It wasn't a tent city any longer. The stores were all made of wood, even if unpainted, and all had proud glass windows, brought in from Spokane Falls on the new railroad. There were sidewalks on the main street and, of course, the two mansions, which were nearly completed. The framework for the fine new Storkersen Restaurant and Café was finished, and only waited for the sides to be nailed on. All in all, Wallace was quite grand and permanent, I thought to myself.

Something caught my eye as I looked out. The streets were empty, for everyone in Wallace was inside Dutch Frank's, but there was something moving down at the end of the street by our old restaurant tents. Jemmy was running toward us, carrying the boxes of giant powder. I watched in amazement as he came up and dumped them into the middle of the street right in front of Dutch Frank's.

"Mr. Gordon, come here quick!" I yelled.

Mr. Gordon turned away from talking and joking with Montana Bellows, put down a sandwich he'd been eating, and came over to me. "Well, little lady," he said, "you sound upset."

"Look!" I cried, pointing out the window.

"Oh, my God!" he breathed. "That's giant powder. What does he think he's goin' to do with it?"

"I think he's going to fire off a wedding salute to all of you," I replied.

"He'll blow us all to kingdom come," he said, sprinting for the door, just as Jemmy opened the second box.

People inside Dutch Frank's place milled over to the window for a better look at what had caused the bridegroom to leave in such a hurry.

Mama called out, "Ann Katie, what's wrong? Where's your brother?"

"He's going to shoot off a firecracker for you, Mama," I called back.

"There ain't no firecrackers up here any more. It's way past the Fourth of July," Helga said, puzzled.

"Holy Saints preserve us!" shouted O'Neil, peering out the window too. "The kid's using giant powder, and I don't think Luke's going to make it in time. Get back from this window fast, everybody."

Everyone rushed away, nearly trampling me, and I fell flat on the floor, tearing my new dress, but not before I saw Jemmy light a long wooden match and throw it into the powder. Then he ran like a rabbit. Luke Gordon ran, too, diving under the high sidewalk.

What a mighty explosion that was! They heard it all the way to Fort Sherman, people told us afterwards. There had never been such a firecracker in the history of the Coeur d'Alenes. Every inch of Wallace shook, and every glass window in the town shattered that day. Dutch Frank's fine new window flew into a thousand pieces, showering all over the people gathered in the saloon. I was covered with flying glass, but, oddly enough, there were almost no cuts and bruises from the fragments. We'd had just warning enough to take cover, falling onto the floor and hiding under saloon tables and chairs.

"Jemmy!" Mama screamed the second after the explosion. "Where is my baby boy?"

I peered out the empty window frame. Jemmy was standing in the middle of the street once more, gazing at all the broken windows, a dazed look on his face, his mouth wide open. Then he spied Mr. Gordon crawling out from under the sidewalk. One look was enough. In a flash he was off, running toward Thompson Falls, with Luke Gordon hot on his heels. I told Mama that Jemmy was fine and unhurt, because I knew he couldn't be hurt when he could run that fast.

The street was a madhouse in less than half a minute. Everyone streamed out of Dutch Frank's, forgetting the champagne in their hurry to calm down their teams and saddle horses. The horses had gone wild, of course. Teams were tangled up in their traces, and were plunging and rearing. Gentle saddle ponies had pulled free from the hitching posts, and were galloping up and down the street. Wedding guests ran around trying to catch the ends of the reins as their horses dashed by, rearing and striking out in terror with their front hoofs. All was confusion for some time.

"Where's Mr. Gordon?" called Mama, coming out on the sidewalk with everyone else, her forehead wrinkled with worry, her wedding bonnet tipped.

"He's chasing Jemmy," I answered her, "but I think he's too old to catch him."

This is where I was again wrong. By the time the horses were quieted down, Luke Gordon strode back up the main street, dragging Jemmy along with him. He jerked him along right up to Mama. "Well, Mrs. Gordon," he said sternly, chewing on his mustache a bit, "here's your boy!"

Mama was pale but determined. "Mr. Gordon," she said clearly, raising her voice a bit, "he is now *your* boy. Do your duty!"

"Gladly, Mrs. Gordon!" our new stepfather declared, and he proceeded to give Jemmy the best and most needed licking he'd ever had, right there with the whole of Wallace looking on and approving.

Jemmy did not cry, but when it was all over, he looked at Mr. Gordon and Mama and said in a sad way, "I was only trying to make you all happy."

"Is blowing up the town your idea of a good time?" asked Mama. "You have no notion of proper behavior whatsoever any more. I knew this would come of not going to school for so long. Well, now I'm not going to wait for a school to open here. You and your sister are leaving next week for boarding schools in Portland, and there'll be no argument from either one of you. I warned you before."

"I didn't set off the powder!" I cried.

"No matter," said Mama. "You're going to a finishing school, and it's high time, too."

"Well, it's all very fine that you've got your family so well set up," spoke out one of the town's store owners in anger, "but who's going to pay for my big window? It cost me plenty."

"Oh, I'll do that gladly," said O'Neil, laughing. "The lad here gave me the finest wedding I've ever heard tell of, except, of course, back in Ireland. It was a genuine bang-up affair. I'll pay for all the windows. Just present your bills to me, gentlemen. What do you think of this, Helga, my love?"

Helga pursed her mouth and shook her head, her veil and orange blossoms tottering. "It was quite a send-off, I'll say," she replied, "but it could'a sent us all off to heaven before we was ready to go. I think sonny ought to be taught a lesson out'a school. He ought to pay you back during his summer vacations by washin' pots and pans in my eatin' house. What do you think of that?"

Jemmy opened his mouth to protest, but Mama spoke for him. "That will be quite equitable, I do believe. I think three years at a nickel per pan should do it nicely."

"I'll be too old!" wailed Jemmy.

"But think what a great pot-and-pan scourer you'll be at the end of it!" added Mama. "A man of honor always pays his debts, Jemmy."

"Anyhow," reflected my brother, "you can't make Timothy Clover wash dishes. I'm glad of that. I just wish I was a mule too."

And so we went off to boarding school at the same time Mama and Mr. Gordon moved into their new home. Jemmy complained a lot about it, until Mr. Gordon promised to build a special stall for Timothy Clover in the carriage house behind the big yellow house and to take care of him always. I didn't make much of a fuss, for I figured that if Mama thought I should be finished, I should be finished all right. After all, I had to live up to long skirts and bustles.

But I did decide one thing, though. I was coming back to Idaho Territory every vacation, and that was where I was going to settle down someday for good. You bet!

AUTHOR'S NOTE

In a way, *Bonanza Girl* really happened.

Perhaps the people in the story (with one or two exceptions, such as Calamity Jane and Andrew Pritchard) aren't real people, but just about everything else is true.

Andrew Pritchard discovered gold in the Coeur d'Alene mountains of Idaho Territory in 1883, and several years later, when the streams were panned out, other prospectors found silver. To this day, the town of Wallace is one of the most important "silver cities" of the West, and is located near the largest silver-lead mine in the world, the fabulous Bunker Hill and Sullivan.

Eagle City is now a ghost town, but once it was a booming gold camp, full of prospectors, businessmen, saloon keepers, gamblers, "desperate characters," and men of all nations. A particularly interesting feature of this area was that there were so many Americans with foreign backgrounds represented. The Irish and the Swedes played a very prominent part in the early history of this part of Idaho, and some of the wealthiest mines of the Coeur d'Alenes were owned by men of Irish or Swedish background.

It is absolutely true that Eagle City, as well as other towns in the area, hated and feared Chinese. Chinese were actually driven out of the region in the early 1880's, and legend persists that they will never be welcome in the panhandle country of Idaho.

Over fifty years ago Fort Sherman was a bustling army post, and the stagecoach from Rathdrum to Fort Sherman was actually robbed in 1885—notorious gunmen were by no means uncommon in the Idaho gold and silver camps.

Calamity Jane and her troupe came to Eagle City in February of 1884, and although there is no record of it, she could have sampled some of the strange items on the menu of Eagle City's restaurants, such as beaver tail and bear paws, for they were really eaten by the Idaho and Oregon pioneers.

Accounts of the deep snows come out of the Coeur d'Alenes nearly every winter nowadays. Avalanches were not unknown in the steep canyons in the past—

and at least one of them tells a tragic tale of a whole crew of miners being crushed.

As the author of *Bonanza Girl*, I am guilty of some deliberate historical inaccuracies in order to help the story along. I have purposely left the gold camp of Murray, the second real town to be founded in the Coeur d'Alenes, out of the narrative. Instead I have combined many of the true incidents of Murray's early days into the accounts of events in Eagle City and Wallace. This is not to take anything of glory from Murray, but only to make transitions easier in the novel. By rights, the Scott family would have settled first in Eagle City, then in Murray, and finally in Wallace. People moved to follow the strikes. I do not think this is a matter of much importance, however, for the citizens of Eagle City, Murray, and Wallace were all the same people, who were great "pickers up and movers on."

The railroad came to the silver camps of the area in 1887—not in 1886, as I have it—but it is a fact that one railroad of the 1880's was laid on ice and snow, and as the ice and snow melted the engines were stranded when the tracks buckled. This is still a favorite joke of the old-timers of the region.

The Coeur d'Alenes remain today as exciting and interesting as they were in the 1880's. The mining region of north Idaho has never really lost the flavor of the old West, and the history of places, like Wallace, Kellogg, and Burke, after 1890 was even more turbulent, wild, and woolly than it was earlier—but that is another story for another time.

Patricia Beatty
March 1959